Destiny: A Fairy Tale
Copyright © 2011 by Aaron Mahnke

All rights reserved. No part of this book may be reproduced in any form or by any electronic or mechanical means including information storage and retrieval systems, without permission in writing from the author. The only exception is by a reviewer, who may quote short excerpts in a review.

ISBN: 978-1463724962

Cover design by Wet Frog Studios.

DEDICATION

This tale is for my little girls. May you never give up the relentless pursuit of who you were created to be.

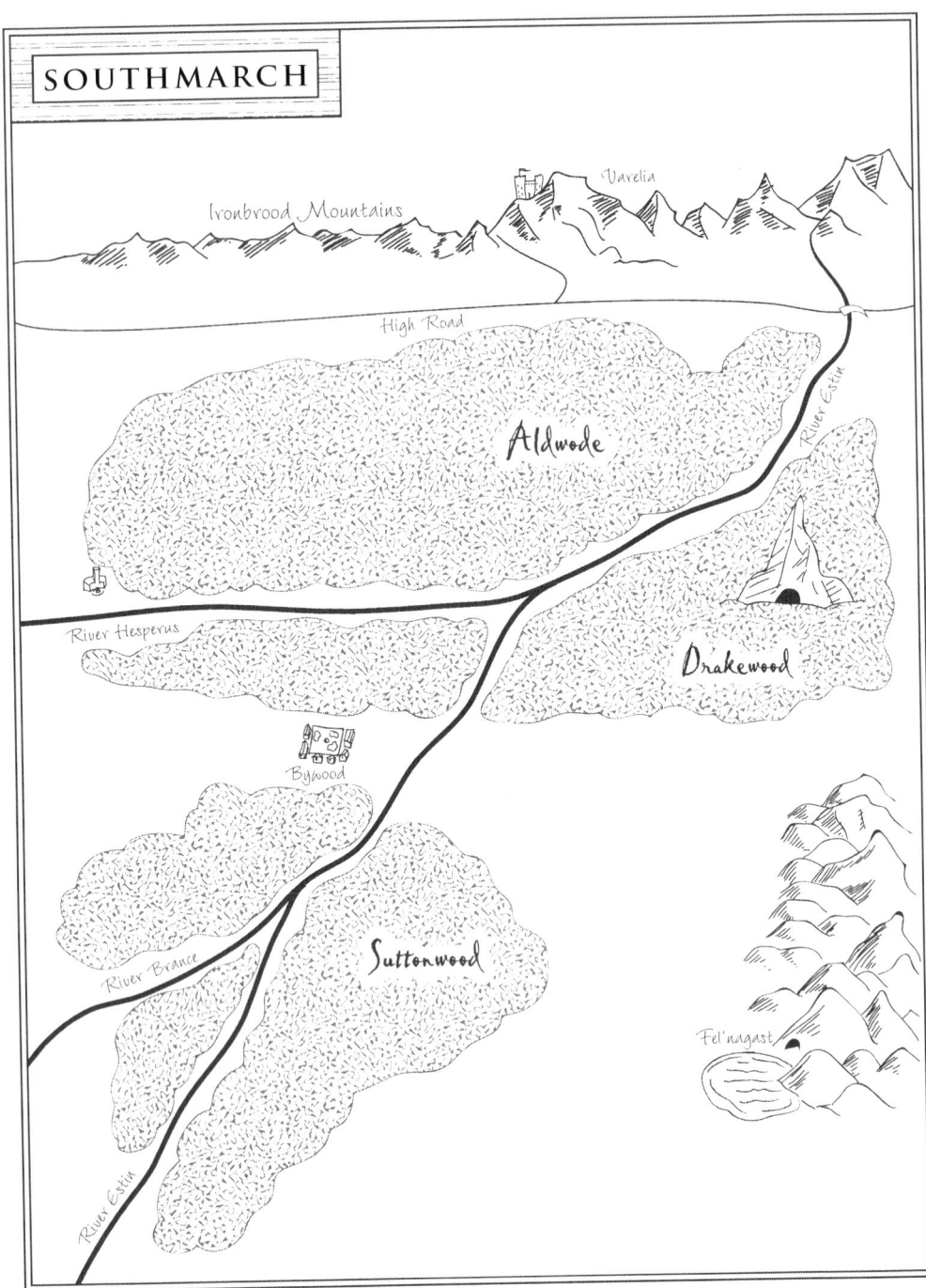

Destiny: A Fairy Tale
by Aaron Mahnke

Chapter 1

Every tale must have a beginning, a birth, a point of departure. Some tales begin long, long ago, while others in a land far away. Some begin with both, and for some, that is where they end as well.

It is said that stories give life to people long dead and forgotten. That the mysterious path to immortality is a life worthy of remembrance. Tales can last thousands of years, or vanish with the coming spring. They can be heirlooms, passed from father to son with love and reverence, or trinkets tossed aside like unwanted toys. Some tales birth gods, and some conceal the truth. This tale does not lay claim to the former, but it certainly deals strongly in the latter. For truth is better digested when taken with honey.

Long ago in a time when the world was younger and full of mystery and wonder, our story took place. Men and women understood that life held more than their eyes were witness to, and powers and allegiances were not always as clear as they first appeared. And that which the people did not understand was what frightened them the most. Life, of course, was difficult enough without mystery and wonder added in.

On the narrow expanse of pastureland between the bright, airy Suttonwood to the south, and the ancient forest of the Aldwode to the north, the tiny village of Bywood reclines in the gentle hills. It was in that place, in Bywood, where our story began.

This tale began in the dead of night, as many tales do, a night of rain and wind and thunderous sounds. It was the sort of storm that filled the air with wetness and wind, lightning and crashing, and an obvious sense that one was better off staying indoors until it was over. So it was with shutters closed and lanterns doused that the citizens of Bywood waited through the night for the full fury of the tempest to pass.

But if anyone had ventured a peak outside of their sheltered abodes, they might have seen, through the shadows and flashes of blue and white lightning, that shapes approached the edge of their humble settlement. Two shapes, to be precise, which seemed to stumble along a small trail that led through the forest to the north edge of the village. The shapes moved slowly, deliberately, but with a sense of haste that was only intensified by the rumbling thunder and flashing light.

The taller of the two shapes was a man, while the smaller was a woman. She moved as one who is oddly burdened, and he seemed to walk carefully, as if the steps pained him. They appeared wet, and tired, and carried very little with them.

The pair entered the village of Bywood from the north, and passed by a handful of shuttered, darkened houses. As they passed through the center of the village, they paused to rest for a moment against a large stone, glistening with each flash of the lightning. The man placed his hand on the stone to steady himself as the woman leaned into him. Her arms were hung low, wrapped around her swollen belly. Her face looked pained.

Both seemed to notice the house ahead of them, the only house with a lamp still burning inside, and they nodded to each other before stepping toward it, slowly and painfully. A crimson handprint where the man had rested against the stone was visible for a brief moment, but the torrential rain soon washed the blood away.

The man did not hesitate to knock on the door of the house, but the beating of his fist seemed to melt perfectly into the rumble of the ominous thunder. The only sound that managed to break through the cacophony was the brief cry of pain from the woman at his side. Her face twisted in agony as she gripped the doorpost with her free hand to hold herself steady.

The man knocked again, harder than before, and suddenly the dim lamplight inside the house began to move, bobbing and swaying, vanishing for a moment and then reappearing once more. And then the door opened, cautiously, slowly.

"What do you want?" questioned a firm, young voice from the darkness of the house. A soft yellow glow cast light on the bare arm and tunic of a man slightly shorter than both the strangers. "The hour is late, and my young family is long abed."

"We seek shelter, good sir," replied the damp and hunched man, his voice strong but gentle. "Please, may we pass the stormy night under your roof?"

"We have no room," the villager offered

curtly, and made to shut the door. The strange man reached out with a trembling hand and stopped the door before it fully closed.

"Please," he pleaded, loud enough for his voice to carry over another long rumble of thunder. "My wife is with child. The birth pains have already begun. We need only a dry shelter and perhaps a midwife if you know of one."

The door slowly reopened, and the yellow light of the lamp moved up as the villager raised it to his face. A young but stern face, with set jaw and taut skin, stared out from the house. When he spoke, his eyes flashed with displeasure.

"Very well," he said through clenched teeth. "But I cannot feed you. We are a poor family with too many hungry bellies as it is. And any payment for your lodgings will be appreciated."

The strange pair stepped through the threshold of the house as the man pulled the door open wide. As the mysterious visitors left the howling wind and biting rain, the man reached out with his bloody hand and gripped the bare arm of his new host.

"I will leave you with the greatest treasure I can offer, you can be sure," he replied, locking eyes with the shorter man. "Now, fetch us aid if you would. My wife has little time left."

With a cold nod, the villager vanished into the darkness of the house, taking the yellow glow of the lamp with him. Within moments, the house seemed to come alive, the sounds of other feet thumping on the floorboards, and the light of more lamps pouring around hidden corners and doorways. Hushed voices, full of urgency and distress, began to fill the air between claps of thunder.

A woman rushed by the pair of strangers, her face too young to look so old, and a small bed was made in the front room of the house. Little was said as the pregnant woman was ushered to the cot and gently laid on her back. Thunder crashed outside again, and the walls seemed to shake as the lightning flickered through the windows.

The man of the house returned with a pail of water and a bundle of clean rags tucked under his arm. His silent wife took one of the rags and dipped it into the water before pressing it to the forehead of the woman on the cot. Water trickled slowly down her brow, mingling with tears and sweat.

"She is nearly ready," said the stern

woman, no emotion visible on her tired face. "There is something wrong with the child, I fear. It pains her too much for my liking."

The tall stranger stepped toward his wife, concern and anxiety painted across his face like a festival mask. He stumbled as he neared the cot, and the younger man caught him by the arm. When he let go, the villager's hands were covered in blood, thick and dark in the dim light.

"You are injured!" he exclaimed, though it was unclear whether he was concerned for his visitor, or for the mess that was being made of his front room. "Let me tend to your wounds, sir."

"I am of no consequence," the stranger said, dismissing the offer with a wave of his hand. "She is my only concern, the center of my world, the heart of my heart."

He sat down beside her and pressed the damp cloth to her brow as she moaned in pain and took sharp, quick breaths. She reached out and took his hand in hers. He smiled at her gently, fiercely, deeply.

At that moment the thunder crashed again, deeper and longer than before, and lightning filled the mottled glass panes of the windows with a white glow. The woman on the cot cried out in extreme pain, and the housewife at her feet tended her with palpable apprehension.

And then came the pushing, the guttural moans and the cries. The stranger's wife seemed to focus all of her will and strength into her task, and the housewife spoke calming words and guided her. The wounded stranger leaned against the wall, one hand holding his bloody side and the other his wife's tightly curled fingers. The austere villager stood back in the shadows, his jaw set like stone. And then, all was quiet.

There was no more thunder, no more howling wind, no more incessant pounding of rain upon roof. For a brief moment, there was no more moaning or crying. Then, like an intense light in a darkened room, a shrill cry rang out. A piercing cry. An infant's cry.

A moment later, the housewife held up a small bundle in the dim lamplight, swaddled in rags and slick with blood. The wounded man grimaced as he leaned toward her, letting go of his wife's limp hand to reach for his newborn child. He took the infant in his trembling hands, and tried to hush it with soothing sounds. Then he turned to his wife, the joy beyond apparent on his beaming face.

"A son," he sighed with exhausted triumph. "We have a son."

But his wife did not stir. She lay as still as stone on the cot in the corner of the darkened room. Tears still glistened in the corners of her eyes, but those eyes were now lifeless and empty. As the new father grasped the meaning of her silence, his eyes too filled with tears. He stood quietly and deliberately, and strode across the room to the young villager in the shadows.

"She was his only hope," he whispered hoarsely, glancing over his shoulder at his wife's form amongst the jumbled bedding. Then he looked back at the young man, and his eyes came alive with resolve and fire.

"Hold him please," he commanded more than he asked, and the stern, dispassionate man reluctantly took the bundled infant from the stranger. "I as well am not long of this world, and shall join my love beyond the veil shortly. But there is still much to accomplish before I pass."

Reaching into his tunic, the wounded man produced a large key, dull gray and cold, and removed the chain that held it from around his neck. He then placed the chain over the newborn's head, and bent low to kiss him on the brow.

"His name shall be Simon," he stated firmly, as he reached out a bloody hand and gripped the shorter man on the shoulder. "The key is his inheritance and his birthright. Keep it safe, as safe as you will keep him. For I am leaving you, as I said I would, with my greatest treasure. Care for this child as you do your own."

The dour villager made to argue, but the stranger stepped quickly away, back toward his wife's lifeless body, and bent low to lift her up. He carried her cradled in his arms, moving without words toward the door. He was in great pain, as was clearly written on his face – the pain of his wounds, the pain of his loss, and the pain of his task. But despite the pain, he opened the door to the cool damp night air.

"But what of the child?" called out the man of the house, the infant held in his outstretched hands, as one would hold an unwanted gift. "You cannot leave him here, with us, for good! We are but a poor family with too many mouths to feed. Please, good sir. Let us tend your wounds and nurse you back to health. For your son!"

"My son needs a father. A family." The wounded man shook his head slowly. "No, I am beyond your help, however noble it is of you to offer. I must see that my wife is buried properly before it is too late."

"But..." the frowning man offered, but then he stopped. The stranger was already gone, leaving only the open door and an eerie silence.

As that silence filled the dimly lit room, the newborn's shrill, piercing cry began anew, followed by the storm, renewed and refreshed in strength. Rain fell hard and thunder clapped loudly, shaking the room, while lightning illuminated the town center beyond the door with a flash of white light. And for a brief moment, in the square at the north side of the village, one dark stranger could be seen stumbling away where two had traveled before.

Chapter 2

By most standards you or I would be used to, Simon had a difficult childhood. Being one of nine children brings with it its own set of challenges. It was hard enough for Mr. Eustace Kendrick to enjoy the thought of feeding and raising the eight children he fathered, but Simon was not even his own son. This simple fact made Mr. Kendrick bitter. And more than a little spiteful.

Mr. Kendrick was a cobbler, known throughout the village of Bywood as an exceedingly frugal man. He dressed all of his children the very same way he and his wife dressed themselves; plain garments cut from rough fabric of muted colors. All of the children were silent in his presence, and as well-mannered as frightened foals. Their well-behaved persona, however, only existed when their father was near. Left on their own they were prone to excitement and unsettled liveliness. All of them, except of course for Simon.

Even though he was only one of many

children in the Kendrick home, Simon often found himself completing his sibling's chores as well as his own. It was not that he volunteered to take them upon himself, but that the rest of his siblings often came to a group decision that left him with more than his share to accomplish for the day. Washing filthy pots and scrubbing dirty floors were tasks in which Simon became very proficient. Never proficient enough, however, to please his mother, Mrs. Elisbeth Kendrick, who held her standards at such a height than no one but herself ever hoped to attain them.

Once, for his ninth birthday, Simon received a single present; a used straw broom, the ends still broken and crusted with stale porridge. He used it that very same day, right after he had made all of the beds and cleaned all of the pots from the morning meal. But most of his birthdays arrived without presents. His parents told him they did not have enough coins for a gift, but it did not take many years before Simon realized the true meaning behind those words.

His parents denied him much during his childhood, usually out of spite or bitterness at the offense of having an orphan imposed upon them, though sometimes because the family was honestly very poor. Of all the things that Mr. and Mrs. Kendrick withheld from Simon, the most tragic neglect was in not telling him of his origin, the tale of his birth and induction into the Kendrick family. In their opinion it was better for the boy to believe he was theirs and unwanted, rather than the child of other parents who, though evidently loving, were lost to him.

The aspect of Simon's home life that brought him the most harassment, though, was his appearance. While the other eight children seemed to be miniature versions of their father, with plain brown hair and tanned skin, Simon was pale as cream, and his head was crowned with a mess of black hair. While all his siblings looked on the world with muted brown eyes, his were a chill blue, like bits of ice from a winter snowstorm. That he stood nearly a head taller than other children his age only seemed to draw more unwanted attention to his shockingly divergent appearance.

Somewhere around his thirteenth year, Simon began to notice the girls of his village, and one girl in particular: Margaret Chilton. Golden haired and fair skinned, she was revered among boys who knew about such things as the most beautiful girl in Bywood. She was certainly not plain by the standards one would judge plainness, and the attention she garnered only secured her reputation. As a boy who spent his life standing out from his peers, Simon was drawn to her singularity. There could be no one else for him but Margaret Chilton.

Margaret Chilton, however, had other ideas about her destiny. She, it seemed, was in love with Alfred Horsham, the son of the village magistrate. He was handsome and genteel, a younger version of his respected father, and dressed in colors that would cause Mrs. Kendrick to blush if they crossed her sewing table. The remarkable Margaret Chilton had been specially chosen by fate to walk home from school with Alfred Horsham.

Fate, it appeared to Simon Kendrick, had no such glorious plans for him.

Most folk who lived in Bywood had done so for a very long time; some were able to recount nearly twenty generations of their family in some cases. And for as long as anyone who was old enough to remember *could* remember, each spring was ushered in with a festival. It was a small celebration compared to those of today, and visitors from beyond the boundaries of Bywood were rare, but it was a joyous occasion, and cause for much excitement normally absent from the quiet village.

At the start of May, as the cool remnants of winter drifted further away, daylight and warmth returned to the land. The farmers of the village no longer woke to a white, crisp layer of frost on the budding leaves of the trees outside their homes. Their breath no longer hung in the air like mist from a lowland stream. As May arrived, so did life, and an annual festival was held to celebrate its return.

The festival itself was a burst of energy, noise, laughter and music. Residents of the village would gather at noon on the day of the celebration and share a large, generous meal together in the square across from the Foxglove Inn. The large grassy expanse was well suited for holding gatherings. The few trees that grew in the square were along the edges, hedging in the tables and booths that the townsfolk had erected. Ribbons of colored fabric had been strung from the branches, connecting one tree to the next. And in the center of it all was the Maidenstone.

The Maidenstone was a massive egg-shaped piece of granite that stood upright from the center of the green expanse. Nearly as tall as a well-fed child, and twice as wide at the base, the stone had no markings on its surface save for a fist-sized hole directly on top, cutting deep into the center of the rock. It was in this hole that the townspeople placed a tall pole of supple yew, and tied more than a dozen strips of white cloth to its top end. The other ends of the fabric were, for the moment, anchored to the grassy ground around the stone, and the slack flowed and rippled in the breeze.

The morning of the festival was full of bustle and busyness. Mr. Blackstone, the owner of the general store, was nearly overwhelmed by all of the orders the people of the village had placed for goods for the celebration. Women moved in and out of his shop like insects upon a piece of half-eaten fruit, approaching the store with empty hands and leaving with heavy burdens. Children ran playfully across the grassy field while mothers chastised them for shirking their chores.

The sound of hammers echoed from the square as many of the town's men gathered to construct the various platforms and benches that would serve the people through the rest of the day.

The late morning air was cool on the skin, and standing on the front porch of one of the buildings set across from the square was Simon Kendrick. The building was oddly shaped, having the structure of a house on one side, and the less attractive form of a shack attached to the other side. Mr. Eustace Kendrick preferred to work where he lived, and so he had long ago built his shoe repair shop directly onto his home. The result was the perfect excuse for a father of nine children to put all of them to work.

So as any seventeen year old son of a spiteful cobbler would be asked to do, Simon had been tasked with delivering a freshly repaired pair of women's riding boots to one of the matrons at the inn. Mrs. Hartford managed the handful of rooms that made up the inn's network of lodging, and had done so for as long as Simon could remember. But as much as she was a domineering inn keeper who demanded perfection from the young women who cleaned the rooms and the old men who tended the stables and baggage, she was also known for her passion for gaudy, overly expressive clothing. Simon was sure that the boots he was now delivering to her would leave no doubt she was still a connoisseur unparalleled.

On his way to the inn he was passed by another small group of young women, some the same age as himself, speaking softly among themselves. A few of them giggled nervously as Simon passed by, but though Margaret Chilton was among them, she was not one of those who laughed. Simon attempted to make eye contact with her, but her attention was firmly leveled across the square where the tall form of Alfred Horsham could be seen among the workers. Disappointment washed over Simon's heart and he bent his head slightly lower and pressed on to the inn. He had been certain that he and Margaret were destined to be together, but every day left him with less hope than before. Perhaps the mood of celebration and revelry brought in by the Spring Festival would nudge Ms. Chilton gently in his direction.

The door of the inn held back the smell of fresh stew and spilled ale, and it quickly presented itself as Simon entered. It was darker inside than he expected, and little light broke through the few small windows that dotted the wall to the left. The handful of small round tables that filled the dining area each held a small candle that emitted weak, yellow balls of light. All of the tables were empty except one, far off in the corner, where a man with broad shoulders sat while Mrs. Hartford stood beside him, talking loudly and laughing dramatically.

Mrs. Hartford was a large woman with a round face and a flat, upturned nose. Her husband had died six summers before, leaving her the Foxglove to care for on her own, which she threw herself into without inhibition. Some assumed it was because she felt great passion for hosting travelers in her establishment, or that she held the position of proprietress in high regard, but most knew that it was at the very least a means of escape from her loss.

Mrs. Hartford stopped speaking with the visitor when she noticed the slight form of Simon slip in through the doorway. The cheerful expression she had worn so convincingly only a moment before was tossed aside like a useless tool.

"It's about time, boy," she barked at him discourteously. "Bring it here."

Simon handed her the package, the brown paper making a soft hissing noise as she pulled it out of his hands. Her fat fingers tore at the wrapping and pried the lid off the large box and and then gasped in wonder at the contents within.

"What fine work your father does," she

cooed softly as she brushed her hand over the stained leather and fine detail of the boots, as fresh and clean as if they were newly bought. "A shame, really, that all he can rely on you for is to transport them."

Simon lowered his gaze. He was used to such treatment, as most of the townsfolk who liked and respected his father had a natural disdain for him. He passed the awkward moment searching the floor for signs of the previous evening's events, noticing the large crumbs from a dry loaf, and one stray glass bead stuck between two of the planks.

"I must put these on at once," she exclaimed as she gathered the box up in her arms. "You may go."

With a speed that seemed unnatural for a woman her size, Mrs. Hartford walked briskly toward the back room doorway. Simon glanced around and found the visitor still at his table, only now he was twisted around and looking carefully at the young man.

"Come here, lad," he requested with a voice that was both gentle and commanding.

Simon shuffled over to the stranger. The man was older than his father by a good few years, but not yet too aged to call old. His dark brown hair was greying, and covered his head in a tangled mess of thick locks, and his broad shoulders were supported by an even broader torso, a memorial to many vanquished meals, it appeared. But it was his long, curled mustache that caught Simon's attention.

"Sit," the man said. His mustache bounced slightly as he spoke, like the springs that Simon had seen at the shop of Mr. Tanner, the local blacksmith. "She wasn't very friendly to you, was she?"

"No sir," he replied mannerly.

"Sir Montgomery Lovelace, at your service," he said, extending a firm hand to the young man. "Knight, adventurer and seeker of all that is fair and just."

Simon shook the man's hand. It was strong, but soft.

"Do you let everyone treat you as such, lad? If anyone spoke to me that way, let alone a woman, I would give them more than a piece of my mind, believe me. What's your name?"

"Simon, sir." He rarely met strangers. More uncommon still was a stranger who had interest in speaking with him. This man was oddly comforting with his dignified strength and tempered respect.

The older man looked Simon over, inspecting him like Mrs. Hartford would a new dress. It made him a bit uncomfortable, and he fiddled with the chain around his neck out of nervousness.

"I take it you're the son of a cobbler, judging from what Mrs. Hartford said as well as what you are wearing." The knight smiled warmly at him. "My father was a cordwainer in Varelia long ago. He made fine items that were sought after by the nobles and well-off citizens of the city. But it was a difficult, taxing occupation that rewarded him with ill health and an early death."

Simon's face darkened slightly, and took on a worried expression, and he tugged anxiously on his necklace. Sir Lovelace caught himself before continuing, and apologized. "Forgive me, that was rude. I'm sure your father will live a long life and find great success through his impeccable cobbling."

"Thank you, Sir Lovelace," Simon responded, letting go of the chain and glancing around the room.

"What is that under your shirt that you are toying with, lad?" the man asked.

"A necklace, sir. One I've had for a very

long time."

"Ah," the knight replied as if understanding. "Can I see it?"

Simon thought to himself for a moment, wondering if he could trust the stranger, or if he was somehow about to be taken for a fool and robbed of the one possession he cherished more than any other. On the other hand, this man was a knight, well-travelled and seemingly honorable. So he took the risk and tugged the chain up from his collar, and held it up for the man to see.

Hanging from the end of the old iron chain was a key. It was not ornate, or even overly large, but it was thick and appeared strong for something so insignificant. It was the color of coal, though under the tarnish Simon was sure the key must be brighter, like an old steel blade. And etched into the surface of one side of the key in rough but ornate script was a single word: destiny.

"It is lovely," the knight declared. His eyes and face belied any emotion, but he did not reach for it or ask to hold it, and that made Simon feel safe. "You say you've had it long, eh?"

Simon nodded. "Yes sir."

Sir Lovelace smiled kindly. "Well, thank you for the honest company, lad. However grateful

I am for the hospitality of Mrs. Hartford, she can give the impression of being more than a little counterfeit in her attempts to make conversation."

Simon nodded again, this time allowing himself to smile slightly. It was nice to hear others say the things he never felt free to say so himself.

"Tell me," the knight said, standing up from his seat, "I am acquainted with no one else in the village, but have been invited to participate in the events of this afternoon's festival. Might I ask to sit near you, so I may have some friendly company with whom to pass the time?"

Simon found the idea to be wonderful, and nodded in agreement. Perhaps seeing him share a table and conversation with a knight would be just what he needed to catch Margaret Chilton's attention. "Of course, Sir." Then, hoping to respond in a manner the knight must be accustomed to, he added, "it would be an honor."

"Wonderful!" the old knight exclaimed with a loud guffaw. "I shall find you in the square later today, then. Good day!" And with that, he turned and left through the front door. Simon, already late in returning to his father's shop, made haste as well, with hopeful thoughts of the Spring Festival taking root in his mind.

Chapter 3

Simon could hear the noise from the square as he stepped outside his home. Fragments of music drifted through the air and he moved quickly toward the source. His path to join the festivities took him a short distance toward the Foxglove, and as he approached he saw the large, imposing figure of Sir Lovelace step out of the front door.

"Simon, my lad!" he exclaimed with a chuckle. "Fancy meeting you again so soon. I blame fortune and destiny. She's always good to us, is that not right?" The older man smiled and smacked him on the back with a chuckle.

Simon nodded, though it was more out of a willingness to be friendly than agreement. Explanations such as fortune and fate were never topics that he entertained. He was a practical young man, or at least as practical as his parents could convince him to be. Like most young men Simon still held on to a small remnant of wonder and hope that something bigger than the harsh reality of village life awaited him. But that remnant was slowly slipping away along with his childhood.

"Tell me more about this festival," said Sir Lovelace. "As a passing traveler I am honored to participate, but would greatly enjoy knowing exactly what it is we are celebrating."

"Well," Simon replied, "we are celebrating the arrival of spring. Our village has done this for as long as anyone can remember. Spring brings new life, and so we celebrate the hope and beauty that comes with it."

"Wonderful," remarked the knight. "The land is filled with far too many opportunities to witness decay and death and the passing of things. So may the festival help us forget our troubles and find hope, my lad!"

They crossed the street and stopped at the edge of the square, and Simon motioned toward the scene that awaited them. "Part of the celebration is the big feast," he said with a wave of his hand, "and of course there are games of skill and chance to pass the time as well."

The large grassy square at the center of the village had been filled with tables for feasting, booths for games and even a small tent had been raised in order for Mr. Crabtree's tavern to serve ale to those who were thirsty for something more than water. The air was filled with excitement, and the wind carried scent of the dozens of foods that had been prepared for the event.

"Judging by the wondrous treats I smell, this might very well be my favorite part of the festival." The knight took a deep, satisfying breath and smiled like a child. It was clear from his waistline that Sir Lovelace knew his way around a feast, and Simon did not doubt his proficiency.

"There is also music and song and dance," he added, pointing toward the large platform near the center of the square where a handful of musicians were practicing a ballad for a later performance. "That is my favorite part," he grinned.

"Oh? And why is that?"

Simon blushed. "The dancing, of course." He pointed to the large stone at the center of the festival. "That is the Maidenstone. The maidens dance around it."

Sir Lovelace hummed with recognition. "I see. I take it there is one maiden in particular who holds your fancy?"

"Perhaps." Simon shifted nervously under

the knight's gaze. "The dance of the maidens is an ancient tradition here in Bywood. Each unmarried woman of age gathers around the stone, takes hold of a streamer and dances. During the dance the young men of the village approach, and each maiden chooses whom she would like to dance with. To be chosen by a maiden, well..."

"I am sure it is a blessed feeling, young lad," suggested Sir Lovelace. "And I am inclined to believe that you have your hopes set on being chosen tonight. Let us hope the Fates smile upon you, then."

Simon squirmed a little more under the questioning, but something this obvious was certainly hard to disguise. What young man could not be in love in the spring? And at the cusp of an annual dance with the village's most beautiful young maidens, at that.

"Simon, my lad," began Lovelace, who then slapped the young man on the back with a broad hand, "you are in good company tonight. For I shall teach you everything you need to know to woo that girl and claim her heart. Come! Let us feast!"

Simon could not tell if he had just been cursed or blessed, but he stepped toward the square and followed Sir Lovelace toward the sounds of music and laughter with a glimmer of hope clutched in his heart.

The music was good and the food was even better. Or at least that is what Sir Lovelace had told Simon a half dozen times over the past hour. The knight, he claimed, had heard better music in the courts of Varelia in his days in the service of the Iron King. But the food was wonderful, according to the man's well-travelled tastes, and he was very clear about his opinion.

"This food is wonderful," he shouted once more over the sound of the music, "and I have very well-travelled tastes."

Simon nodded and took another bite of the roast mutton that he had been working on since arriving. The knight had paid for a wonderful meal for them both from one of the booths, and he did not wish to appear ungrateful by eating it too quickly. Sir Lovelace, on the other hand, stood up and made his way back over to where the food was being served. It was his third trip, so he knew the way quite well.

"There you are," came the sound of a

bitter voice behind him. Simon turned to see his father and mother approaching, their faces twisted in the manner of someone who had just eaten a lemon whole. Mrs. Kendrick was outpacing her husband, and shot Simon a blistering glance. "Why are you not sitting with your family for the meal?"

The young man opened his mouth to reply, but his father caught up and joined the discussion. "Answer your mother, boy. Where have you been?" His father resembled an oversized possum when he got angry, and his slightly prominent front teeth did not help remedy the similarity at all.

"I've been here, with Sir Lovelace," he replied as innocently as he could manage. It was true that he should have been feasting at his family's table, but he felt he was doing the right thing by entertaining the visiting knight. Someone had to do it. "He's a knight of the realm, passing through Bywood on his journey, and he needed to be shown around and kept company during the festival."

"Why, you little..." his mother began before stopping. Her face was becoming more red every moment. Simon did not like where this was headed. "We brought food for you and made the rest of the family wait until you arrived before beginning their meal. You are a rude and selfish child!"

"Pardon me," came the calm voice of Sir Lovelace from behind them, the look on his face both peaceful and concerned. "What seems to be the trouble, madam?

"Madam?" Simon's mother wheeled around to greet the speaker with another serving of her wrath, only to find a stranger looking at her. Sir Lovelace's calm expression seemed to abate her anger for a moment, but it did not dissipate. "My son failed to join his father and I for the feast, and we have come to take him home."

"You're taking me home?" Simon cried out. "What have I done to deserve missing the rest of the festival? I've played host to an honored guest. Besides, if I leave now, I'll miss my chance to dance with the maidens."

The knight stepped between Simon and his parents slowly and without a threatening gesture, and then joined the conversation. "Where I am from, among the nobles and royalty of Varelia no less, your son would be considered a well-mannered lad with good intentions. I apologize if I have kept him from upholding his obligation to your family this evening, and I take full responsibility for that mistake. But your son has been a courteous and polite host to this lonely traveler, and for that I am grateful. Please, if it would be possible, allow the lad to remain here and keep me out of harms way. I fear I may over indulge without his restraining guidance."

Sir Lovelace smiled beguilingly as if Simon's mother were a maiden of the court and he her suitor. For a moment Simon wondered if the knight had accomplished anything other than to fan the flames of his mother's fury, but something in her face slowly softened.

"Fine," she spat, though less venomous this time. "He can stay with you." Then, turning her gaze toward her son she raised a long, sharp finger and leveled it at him. "But I expect you home no later than sunset. Am I understood, boy?"

Simon nodded without a word, afraid to destroy the peace that Sir Lovelace had somehow managed to conjure from thin air and then balance on the edge of a vast precipice. Mrs. Kendrick turned on her heels and stormed resolutely from their table, followed dutifully by her husband. And as abruptly as it had begun the incident was over.

"Lad," began the old knight, "your mother is a woman of unsurpassed passion and irrationality. I have faced many a fierce foe in my time, but I was more afraid for my life in that moment than I have been in years." And then, with a smile and a wink, he added, "Let us return to our feast!"

The western sky was painted a mixture of rose and yellow as the musicians shifted the mood of their casual tune to something more lively. As if on queue the villagers all began to clap to the rhythm of the song. Someone in the crowd whistled the familiar tune loudly.

Before the first measure was done, a dozen or more of the most beautiful young ladies of Bywood had left their seats and gathered around the base of the massive Maidenstone. Each took up one of the long strips of white fabric in hand, and began to dance. They skipped and turned, dipped and swung, their festival gowns flowing with each movement. And all the while the Maidenstone remained at their center as the white cloth rotated around the pole that protruded from its pinnacle.

Simon watched with a combination of reverence and longing as the young maidens moved and danced before him. He did not have to look long before his eyes settled on Margaret Chilton, the desire of his heart and center of his hopes. She spun in a small circle while passing around Simon's side of the Maidenstone. Her hair was like ribbons of gold flowing behind her, or like sunlight trailing the chariot of a goddess. Simon felt himself leaning forward.

After two rotations around the pole and stone a number of the young men stood from their seats and made their way toward the dancing maidens. Simon watched Alfred Horsham rise and step forward, and instinctively did the same.

This was the moment he had been waiting for, his chance to dance with the girl he loved. He cast a quick glance at Sir Lovelace, who smiled wide and joined the rhythmic clapping. Then, Simon moved closer.

Margaret's path had brought her around the stone again. Simon extended his hand as he neared her, reaching for hers. It was like trying to capture a flying bird, her arms moved so quickly and gracefully. But Simon saw two hands reaching for her. The other belonged to Alfred. And as their hands inched closer to the dancing Margaret, she reached out and grasped one of them.

It was not Simon's. It took what seemed

like centuries to reach her, and within a matter of seconds she was pulling Alfred into her arms and spinning away with him. The smile on her beautiful face and the bounce to her step made it clear that she had chosen the hand she desired. And in that moment Simon fully realized that Margaret would never choose him.

Laughter and cheers erupted from the townspeople and dancers as the music grew louder and more urgent. They were clapping harder now, beating out the rhythm as the energy built up. And Simon stood still amidst the motion, his world full of darkness and shattered hopes. And then the familiar face of Margaret made the turn from the far side of the Maidenstone once more, only this time with Alfred by her side, and Simon stepped away.

The festival melted away. He crossed the grass of the square in a daze, numb to the world around him. It was all he could do to find his way south through the dimming light, passing in and out of shadows as deep and dark as the night to come. But the quieter the music became, the more aware he was of his surroundings. And in a matter of moments he had reached the street along the southern end of the square.

"Simon," called the familiar voice of Sir Lovelace from somewhere behind him. The young man turned to find the older man walking briskly toward him through the fading light. The man's breath was short and quick, like someone who had run a mile chasing a loose horse.

Simon turned away and walked faster. "Leave me alone," he muttered.

"Lad," the knight pleaded, "there are other women here. Stay and keep me company a while longer. It will do your spirit good."

Simon stopped and shook his head. "No, but thank you, Sir Lovelace." His voice was morose and clothed in defeat. "Good evening, Sir. Thank you for a fine afternoon and may your travels be safe and swift."

"Simon..." began the older man, but Simon turned and crossed the street, heading east to his family home. Sir Lovelace watched him walk for a moment before shrugging and heading back to the festival. But he laughed no more that night.

When Simon stepped through the front door of the small house he was greeted by his parents stern faces. They had apparently settled in front of the small window that looked out on the square to watch for the young man's return. He caught their eyes as he closed the door, and then made quick for the next room.

"Don't be a fool, boy," came the bitter tones of his mother. "We have much left to discuss now that your lofty friend, the brave knight, is no longer standing between us. Sit." She pointed to a short wooden stool near the hearth and then crossed her arms.

It was useless to resist. Elisbeth Kendrick was known the village over as a stubborn, unmovable woman. Most avoided crossing her much like they eluded Mr. Blackstone's cranky old hunting dog. But living in the same house as the woman made evasion difficult.

"I trust you enjoyed the rest of your evening, free from the tethers of responsibility to your family?"

Simon looked at the floor, the pain from his rejection by Margaret welling up like the river after spring thaw. But he kept control of his emotions knowing his mother would twist and turn them like levers in a mill, grinding away at his resolve.

"Margaret Chilton chose to dance with someone else," he stated with no emotion in his voice. He was proud of his self-control, given the circumstances.

Mrs. Kendrick laughed sarcastically, "Dance? Did you really think any of those maidens would dance with you?" Her face almost seemed to express pity, but there was also a hint of bitterness. "Boy, why would you think someone else would care about you, when your own parents barely do?"

"Elisbeth!" It was Mr. Kendrick this time. His possum-like mouth was held wide open in horror. "Do not speak in such a manner to him. You have crossed a line that should not be breached."

Simon's mother, however, did not seem deterred. "You bite your tongue, Eustace. This is as much your fault as it is his. If you had simply told that man you could not care for his miserable infant, we would not be having this conversation. You allowed the boy to stay with us. And your actions have brought strife and struggle on this family for far too long. It is time the boy should know."

Simon felt the numbing darkness swirl around his head again and put out a hand to steady himself on the stone wall of the fireplace.

He did not fully understand what she was suggesting. "Stranger? Allowed me...? What do you mean?" he asked desperately. "I thought I was born right here in this house. What stranger?"

For the first time that afternoon, Simon watched a smile form on the face of the woman he thought was his mother. She slowly turned from her husband and looked at the young man. And then she began.

"You were born in this house, boy, that much is true. But you are no child of ours." She paused to let the words sink in, the corners of her venomous mouth turned up slightly. "A stranger came in the middle of the night and nearly pounded our door down. He forced us to take in his sickly pregnant wife, who proceeded to give birth moments later. And then she died."

He was stunned. Everything he had ever believed about his life, and his parents, was a lie. Simon did not know how to behave, whether he should shout in rage or silently accept the revelation as fact and move on. But his silence appeared to please her greatly, so he interrupted with a question.

"And my father? What became of him?" he asked calmly, his voice shaking slightly with emotion. "Who was my father?"

"How should I know?" she bit back at him. "He was a stranger, and gravely wounded. He disappeared as quickly as he arrived. Abandoned you with us, he did, most likely so that he could crawl off and die. You should be grateful we kept you."

"Elisbeth," said the man Simon had always known as his father. He extended a hand toward her as if to hold her back and prevent her from doing more harm. Then, turning to Simon, he said, "He was gravely wounded when they arrived that night. I offered help, but he refused to let me tend to his wounds. He made it clear that his priority was to see you safely born and placed in the care of someone responsible. He left me no name, and no way to know where he had come from. Only the key."

Simon instinctively reached down to his chest where the old iron key hung heavily against his shirt. It felt as cold as his heart at that moment. He had been lied to and deceived, and his identity had been hidden from him for years by these people. He felt anger and betrayal and loss all at once. And then he stood.

"Good night to you both," he said as calmly

as he could manage. With that, he turned and walked away.

Simon slept on a small cot in the back of the shop connected to the house, and he made his way there in the dark. He could still hear the sounds of the festival through one of the small windows that had been left cracked open. Simon felt his way to the window and looked out. The night had fully descended, but he could still make out the light from the dozens of small torches around the Maidenstone and the gentle spring breeze carried remnants of the music across the square.

He pulled the window shut and the festival vanished. He needed the quiet to think clearly. He had much to consider, and much more to plan. His head was filled with ideas and thoughts as he lowered himself onto the thin, lumpy cot and pulled an old wool blanket over his body.

As Simon laid his head down those thoughts became plans, and the plans became commitments. Before he drifted off he was certain that tomorrow would be the first day of a new chapter of his life. And he would begin the journey by leaving town with Sir Lovelace.

Chapter 4

The Hunter's boot heels echoed across the cold, hard expanse of the granite floor and walls. The sun was beginning to push the first rays of its light up over the edges of the mountains to the east and the air was chill. But the air was always chill in Varelia, especially high up in the lofty palace of the Iron King.

He moved with slow deliberate steps across a wide antechamber. To either side of him, large open windows looked out on the land below. The breeze that pushed through them was strong and it billowed his cloak as he passed through the room.

The Hunter was a tall man by most standards, and powerfully built. Across his broad shoulders draped a long heavy cloak of black wool and oiled leather, trimmed in sable. His clothing was just as dark, and his hands were covered in black leather gloves that appeared to have seen much use. The man was, according to most who witnessed him, dressed plainly enough (if one discounted the lack of color or pattern in his clothing) aside from one obvious detail that stood out.

Upon the Hunter's head sat a dark helm of aged iron from which protruded a pair of very realistic antlers. The helm itself was modestly crafted, but the antlers were perfect in every detail, including the remnants of velvet still clinging to the bone. They were a strong set as well, with a series of sharp tines sprouting upward from a forward-curving main beam, similar to what one might see on the deer of the Aldwode south of Varelia.

The helm was masked with a beautiful rendering of a bearded man's face, which obscured the Hunter's features entirely. The mask was cast in silver and shone like the moon at full might. Not a trace of the Hunter's face could be seen beneath or around its edges. Only his cool blue eyes were visible, piercing through the small openings beneath the brows on his metallic veil.

And this is how the Hunter was seen as he travelled about the lands and the halls of the palace of the Iron King. He was the dark harbinger of imperial wrath, the courier of clandestine correspondence, and the most fearsome swordsman this side of the Ironbrood

Mountains. He answered to no man save the King, and commanded nearly the same level of trepidation and respect.

The Hunter had been summoned by his King moments before by an out of breath servant carrying a sealed letter. Always ready and available, the Hunter had walked quickly from his quarters and through the labyrinthine hallways toward the most secluded and guarded wing of the palace. The antechamber and throne room were built at the highest reaches of the fortress, which itself was set as high up the mountainside as the road would go. And up here the chill air and biting wind had become as familiar to the Hunter as his own home within the stone walls below.

After a long walk across the cold, grey floor the Hunter reached the massive wooden doors set into the wall at the end of the room. They were taller than four men together, and wide enough for a carriage to pass through. The thick oak boards of the door were blackened with age and bound with wide bands of roughly fashioned iron. The Hunter pressed his gloved hands against the doors and pushed firmly, and then stood back to watch as they swung inward with a slow groan.

Warm air pushed out from the room

beyond. The throne sat at the far end in the center of a raised platform beneath a wide arrangement of clerestory windows that let in the dim light of the coming morning. He could see King Telarius perched on the throne, a massive granite and iron structure with spires and metalwork that rose high above the floor. The echos were fainter in the throne room, but the Hunter's boots still left an audible trail as he moved toward his master.

He stopped at the foot of the dais and smoothly lowered himself to one knee, resting his arm on the other and bowing his head low. His antlers reached forward like a withered hand.

"Rise, my Hunter," boomed the voice from above him. He lifted his head and fixed his eyes on the King, and then slowly stood again. "You came quickly."

The Hunter nodded once. He spoke only when it was unavoidable, even in the presence of the King. It was not out of a lack of ability, but simply a desire to remain as silent as the darkness he felt. His master knew this and allowed it, though he occasionally requested more than a nod or a motion and so the Hunter would comply. But more was not necessary in this moment.

King Telarius stood as well and began

pacing the width of the dais. He was an old man, perhaps seventy summers old or more. The Hunter noticed, because that was part of his job to notice things, that the King still looked much as he did when he first came to serve his Master. His hair was still long and grey and held back from his brow by the thin silver band that he wore there. He stood tall, though not quite as tall as the man in black.

"Let me tell you a story," Telarius began. His voice was deep and strong. He walked back to the immense structure of his throne and lowered himself carefully onto the seat. "My ancestor conquered this land. He built this very fortress, in fact. Toren was his name, and he was the first of my ancestors to take up the mantle of the Iron King. We have all ruled with resolve and control befitting our namesake."

The King held up his hands and looked into their empty palms, as if he had lost something that he longed to have back. Then he continued, more energetic than before.

"Toren, though...ah, he was magnificent. He came from the lands north of the Ironbrood Mountains, a land of magic and dragons and battles the likes of which we have never seen since.

And he brought all of the land south of the mountains under his control. This kingdom was once a grand Empire that stretched countless leagues to the east, west and south, and Varelia sat at it's heart, the seat of Toren's power and the symbol of his might.

"The legends tell us that the source of Toren's great power was a crown," he said, reaching up to brush his fingers against the thin band he wore around his head. "A crown that would make this seem as though it were a child's plaything. A crown forged on the anvil of Velentar himself and imbued with the magic of a thousand wizards. Some say Toren stole the crown, and some claim it was a gift. Regardless, that crown brought him great power."

The King dropped his hands into his lap in frustration. "But that crown is lost," he sighed, looking up at the man with the antlered helm. "It seems that Toren did not trust his children to wield the power of the crown and so he hid it away. With the passing of Toren the Empire began to crumble, first from within and then beyond the walls of Varelia.

"Toren's oldest son and heir, Lugus, was killed shortly after by his younger siblings. And as each generation has taken this throne, the Empire has grown progressively smaller. Today I rule from a seat of impotence, ruling over no more than this palace and the town below. I have no heir, having lost a daughter and three sons to the pains of this world long before their time, and I face abandoning the throne should I die tomorrow. I fear that Toren would feel great disappointment toward his descendants were he to return from the grave."

King Telarius then rose from his seat and stepped slowly down from the dais. " Today we begin to repair that which was broken, my friend. Today we will reach out and reclaim this land, and restore the Empire to the glory it once knew. Today," he said loudly, his voice echoing off the vaulted ceiling and countless arches, "you will begin your journey to reclaim the lost crown of Toren. With the crown in my possession I will stave off death, strengthen the throne and return the boundaries of this kingdom to a glory last seen in the days of Toren."

The Hunter nodded. It was his only logical response. He might deem the quest to be nothing more than folly, or find the challenge beyond his skills and experience. But those were doubts that he rarely felt. He was a capable, resourceful man and while the task was not a simple one he felt confident that he would be able to fulfill his master's wish.

The King stepped down to stand before the Hunter's black, cloaked form. His expression was one of a stern father. "You are well-equipped for this journey. But you will need a place to begin. There are few alive today who remember the Empire in its days of glory, but I know you can find those that do."

The King produced a small rolled parchment from the sleeve of his garments. "This map will guide you on your quest."

The Hunter bowed his head, and then took the map from his master. King Telarius caught his arm as he moved to slip the parchment into his black cloak, and looked directly into the eyes of the silver mask.

"Do not fail me," he intoned. "I will not tolerate a Hunter who can be defeated, and I will certainly not tolerate a Hunter who fails. A Hunter can always be replaced." Only then did the King let go.

The Hunter nodded again, and then slowly turned and walked back the way he had come. He had a mission to fulfill now, and needed to make preparations for the journey. But as he walked through the immense wooden doors that separated the throne room from the chamber beyond, a feeling crept over him that he had not felt in many years. Perhaps it was the biting chill of the wind pushing through the windows, or it might have been the cold echo of his boots on stone. But the Hunter was fairly certain the source was deep within himself.

    He was anxious.

Chapter 5

The sun had not yet finished climbing over the horizon when Simon awoke. The dim light reflected his mood, and the chill in the air was made all the more bitter by his thoughts. But Simon needed to make haste and leave the house before his absence was discovered, and so he swung his feet over to the cold floor and felt for his boots.

Simon knew he needed to leave Bywood. He had never truly felt assured that his future would be found here, but the revelations from the night before had erased any doubt he might have had. His path lay beyond the boundaries of this village.

There was a large leather pack under the workbench and he retrieved it quietly. Stepping softly to the cupboard he removed two loaves of hard bread and a block of yellow cheese. Simon filled a large water skin and packed that into the bag with his wool blanket and a warmer change of clothing. Then, after taking one last look around the small corner in the back of the shop that he had called home for years, he stepped out into the chill morning air.

It was silent across the street, and the only signs of the celebration from the previous evening were the dozens of wooden tables still standing around the Maidenstone. Simon stepped down from the shop to the street and quickly made his way across to the cover of the shadows beneath the trees. The square formed the heart of the village, with streets on either side, so it made sense for Simon to cut through the darkness there on his way to the inn.

The only street that did not have any buildings along it was the one along the north side. That side abutted the southern most fringe of the Aldwode, the oldest and most dense woodland in all the land. And even though most of the villagers avoided it, Simon knew that it was the direction he would be heading. His first stop, though, was the Foxglove to find Sir Lovelace.

After walking north up the eastern street he stopped at the front of the inn. A handful of lights were on inside as the servants and cook went about their morning duties in preparation for the day. Rather than walk in the front door, Simon walked around to the back of the building and found the stable near the back entrance. He peaked quickly inside and saw a very tall, elegant white courser stabled near the entrance. Bywood was a small town, so Simon felt fairly confident that it belonged to the visiting knight.

He approached the back of the inn and was about to reach for the door when it slowly inched open, making very little noise at all. Simon stepped back to allow it to swing fully outward and then watched as the wide form of Sir Lovelace eased itself through the threshold.

"Good morning, Sir Lovelace," Simon said cheerfully.

At the sound of Simon's greeting, the older man yelped and stumbled backwards onto the trampled grass between the inn and the stable, dropping the few belongings he had been carrying. He resembled a startled, wide eyed rabbit who had been pulled from its burrow.

"Lad!" the knight exclaimed with more than a little surprise in his voice. As he pulled himself back to his feet he looked around the yard carefully. "Whatever are you doing here?" The man sounded more than a little put off.

Simon was taken aback. It seemed as

though the man he had treated as a friend the evening before was not interested in spending more time with him. It was another blow to his already wounded spirit. He turned to walk away.

"Wait," said the knight. "I apologize. You merely startled me, that is all. I am glad to see you, Simon."

The young man paused and turned back to Sir Lovelace. "Are you leaving so early, Sir?" he asked.

The knight nodded. "I have a long journey ahead of myself this day, with many miles to cover between here and my destination. I plan to seek out and defeat the great dragon known as the Red Drake." Then he stopped and focused on Simon more intently. "Lad, why are you here, and so early in the day?"

Simon looked down at his feet. The grass behind the Foxglove was matted and yellow and never seemed to grow into the green mane that could be found in other yards and all across the square. He kicked at a clump of dried weeds before responding.

"I wish to leave Bywood, and had hopes that I may accompany you on your journey, Sir," he said as politely as he could.

"Leave Bywood?" the knight exclaimed. "Why ever would you leave your home, lad?" He stooped to gather his scattered possessions and steered the conversation toward the stable with a tip of his head. "Do you have your parent's permission to embark on such a quest?"

Simon did not know how to respond or where to start in his explanation, and so he simply shook his head and told the truth. "They are not my parents. They told me last night. I am an orphan, abandoned to their care on the night of my birth."

A look of surprise crossed his face, and then Sir Lovelace placed a large hand on Simon's shoulder. "Lad," he said softly, "I am sorry to hear. You must feel lost, I can understand, but what do you hope to accomplish by leaving your village?"

Simon was quick to respond, "My destiny, Sir." He pulled the key out of his shirt and held it up to the knight. "I wish to discover the meaning behind this key. Perhaps it can tell me who I really am."

The older man thought for a moment, then glanced quickly at the large inn. Someone lit a lantern in one of the lower level rooms, and almost immediately Sir Lovelace turned and stepped into the stable.

"I feel that is an admirable plan, lad," he said hastily. "Help me ready my steed."

The pair stepped toward the stall that held the tall white courser and opened the door. Sir Lovelace guided the horse out into the open space between the stalls and quickly located his saddle. Simon helped him work the straps and buckles around the horse's thick midsection, but as he did he became increasingly aware that the knight was in a hurry.

"What is the matter, Sir Lovelace?" he asked curiously. "You seem to be uneasy and rushed."

The knight glanced out the stable door one more time. He seemed to be searching for the right words to say. "The lady of the inn and I seem to have had a disagreement regarding the cost of my lodging at her establishment." His eyes shifted as he spoke, and he continued to load his belongings onto the horse.

"What sort of disagreement, Sir?" he inquired. The knight seemed to squirm.

"Mind your manners, lad," he shot back sternly, and then relaxed again. "I'm sorry. Truly, we must be leaving at once. Please, help me finish and then I will allow you to join me behind the saddle. Billy is a fine horse, and strong, and should have no problem carrying us both for much of the day."

Simon agreed and abandoned his questions to help the knight complete preparations, and summarily joined him upon the saddle. "Where will we be traveling to today, Sir?" he asked.

"North for a spell, and then east. The dragon I seek calls the eastern edges of the Aldwode home. Some refer to those lands as the Drakewood."

The knight guided his horse out of the stable and around the side of the inn. They moved quietly up to the street, and then turned their direction to the right to follow it north for a short distance. When they reached the street that ran along the northern side of the square, Sir Lovelace steered them east for a moment, and then north again on a small little path that pressed into the fringes of the forest.

Simon had never travelled on this road before, strictly avoiding the forest like most of the residents of the village had for generations. But he had awoken this morning fully aware that he was about to cross the boundary that stood between the familiar and the uncharted, and as his head passed under the first branches of the ancient trees he could not help but hold his breath.

Time passed slowly under the network of twisted, gnarled branches that made up the canopy of the Aldwode. Little light made it through the upper reaches of the trees, giving the area around the trunks of the trees a feeling of perpetual twilight. There was no late morning, or noon, or even a hazy afternoon, but simply one long hour of dusk after another.

Simon was not sure how Sir Lovelace was able to keep time in the isolated depths of the dark forest, but after hours of riding and maneuvering around the twisted roots of hundreds of trees, the knight simply stopped.

"It is time for us to make camp," he declared as he slid from the saddle.

Simon followed quickly, eager to place his feet on solid ground again. His back side was numb from the uncomfortable position he had been in behind a large man on a saddle made for one.

Sir Lovelace pulled a small kit from his saddlebag and held it up to Simon. "This is a flint and steel for starting fires. I will begin a fire for our evening meal, but I need you to go locate a healthy supply of wood to burn."

He bent down and picked up a fallen branch. It was roughly the size and length of an arm, and was visibly dry. "Find me a large armful of pieces such as this," he requested. And then he set about building a small camp around the tree they had stopped beneath.

Simon began to wander around the perimeter of the camp, picking up any branches that seemed to fit the description. Some were too damp and were tossed aside, while others were simply too small. And as he followed the trail he wandered farther and farther away from camp until suddenly he glanced up and realized he could not see Sir Lovelace or the horse any longer.

"Here is a good piece of kindling," said a voice behind him. Simon spun around to find a woman near by, holding out a good sample of firewood.

"Hello," she said as she stepped out of what seemed like thin air, halting Simon in his tracks. Her voice was like honey and her face seemed to glow. "May I join you on your walk?"

She might have asked him, but he failed to

consider it a choice. He nodded politely, and with eyes slightly wider with confusion, and continued on searching for firewood. The woman fell in step beside him and walked silently for a moment before speaking again.

"I am Juno," she stated. "What is your name?"

"Simon," he replied to the strange woman. "I...ah..."

Juno smiled. "It is a pleasure to meet you, Simon."

She seemed confident and strong. But her lithe figure and long, straight auburn hair gave her a youthful presence. Even the air about her did in fact seem to shimmer ever so slightly in the fading light of the afternoon.

"Where..." he began, and then paused, unsure if he should be asking questions of strange women who appeared to travelers in the depths of the Aldwode. "Where did you come from?" He was nervous to hear her answer.

"Ah," she replied, as if he had asked her about a favorite food. "This is my home. The forest. That tree over there, in fact," and she pointed one of her slender hands in the direction of what might have been a dozen trees. "I am a wood nymph."

"A what?" he asked. He was confused and overwhelmed. "You live in a tree? Like a squirrel?"

The woman laughed with a bright, cheerful voice and smiled at Simon. "No, I live in a grove near here. You and your companion travelled slightly closer to my home than I felt comfortable with, so I thought I would come to meet you and see if you were friend or foe."

Simon nodded as if he understood.

"The key you wear around your neck is very old," she pointed to his chest. Simon did not realize that his necklace was not inside his shirt. "It is odd to see something so ancient around the neck of someone so young."

"I have seen seventeen summers," he responded, puffing his chest up to help convince her of his maturity. "I'm not as young as you think."

"Of course," she smiled back. "Dragons love keys. I trust you do not have any plans to visit a dragon?"

Simon was taken aback. "How did you know we were traveling to the Drakewood?" he asked defensively.

The nymph shook her head. "I did not

know, I tell you truly. I merely wished to warn you that there are few things besides keys and gold that dragons love. And they love keys, of course, because they tend to unlock other treasures."

Simon bent down to pick up another large piece of firewood. "Thank you for the warning, then," he offered. "I will keep it safe. I have no plans myself to go near the dragon."

"If I may ask, how did you come to posses such a treasure?"

"This?" he clutched at the key, protecting it from her imaginary grasp. "I've had it since I was a baby. My real father gave it to me. Before he died."

"Oh, I am sorry, Simon." Her face was visibly saddened. "You have lost so much..." her gaze drifted to something behind him.

"Simon, lad?"

Simon turned around to find Sir Lovelace standing behind him. The knight's dagger was drawn, and his face was drawn into a frown, causing him to appear more serious than usual. They locked eyes for a moment before the older man broke the silence.

"Who were you speaking with, lad?" he asked curiously.

Simon turned back to where the woman

had been standing, but there was no longer any sign of her, not even a trace of her footsteps in the leaves. He must have imagined the conversation, or perhaps the fading light of the dark forest was playing some sort of trick on his senses. Whatever the explanation, however, Simon was concerned that Sir Lovelace might deem him unfit to continue on the journey if he suspected something was wrong. And so he chose, for the moment, to lie.

"Oh, just myself," he replied, doing his best to not seem as though he had lost his wit. "I think I have enough firewood now." He held up the large bundle of broken branches and fallen limbs for the knight to see.

Sir Lovelace smiled. "Yes, it seems you do. Let us get these back to our camp," he said, stashing his knife and taking a portion of the wood. "It will be dark soon, and we would not like being without light in this forest. Trust me."

Chapter 6

The Hunter's journey had taken him from the heights of the glorious palace of the Iron King, high up in the Ironbrood Mountains, all the way to the valley below. Where the palace had been wrapped in chill air and sharp breezes, the wide expanse of the foothills was green and lush and bathed in sunlight. The two were connected by a thin, winding, treacherous path known as the High Road. Long and steep, it was rarely taken on horseback as the animals tended to dislike the great heights and dizzying views. And so it was on foot that the Hunter made his way down the mountain, a path he knew well enough to have little fear and traverse in only a handful of hours.

After a laborious descent past the bustling city of Varelia and down the long and twisted High Road, he found his way to the royal stables. Nestled in the crook between two foothills, the King's stables were built along the road that carried on past the hills off into the distance. Apart from the stable there was a smithy, an inn, a guardhouse and a tavern, both for the weary travelers arriving from the lands beyond but also for the few residents of Varelia who chose to wander outside the boundaries of the King's domain.

The Hunter's mount was stabled in a large, comfortable stall near the back of the building, where it was darker. The horse, an intelligent, well-muscled male, was colored as black as the night. Anthus, as he was called, was loyal only to his master, though he tolerated the care of the stable master much like an adult tolerates the advice received from an elderly parent. He was a hard worker, and stronger than most other horses his size, all of which were attributes that the Hunter required.

The sun was already nearing the horizon when he stepped into the stable. Turning to move in the direction of Anthus, a voice from outside called to him.

"Ho, there!" someone yelled. "What do you need in my stable?"

The Hunter turned as an old man stumbled into view. When the stable master looked up to see who had entered the building, his eyes widened and he bowed his head.

"My apologies, Master," he cringed. "I did not recognize you in the dim light. My eyes are failing me, it seems." He kept his face downcast.

"Leave," spoke the Hunter. His voice was strong and deep, though the silver mask he wore caused it to sound more heavy and menacing than it truly was. The old man turned and ran away in a manner that almost seemed to speak of relief.

The Hunter made his way to the stall that held Anthus. In the fading light at the rear of the stable he found his proud mount waiting for him, head held high and muscles stiff. There was a simple saddle of black leather resting on the gate of the stall, and he lifted it, making his way inside.

Anthus was trained to only move when asked, and the Hunter seldom spoke. He placed the saddle on the horse's back and quietly, slowly, fastened the straps. The bridle slipped on easily and the reins were hung over the horn of the saddle. And then the Hunter left the stall.

The horse followed obediently. There was no need to guide him yet, as they were still in familiar territory. All he had to do was walk and Anthus would follow him. This simple act of obedience allowed the Hunter to remain completely aware of his surroundings and alert to any danger or target or moving prey.

He left the stable and walked a short distance to the tavern. While the Hunter did not drink (ale, of course, clouds the mind and reduces alertness), he did require certain supplies from the man who managed the establishment. Anthus stopped following him when he stepped off the stone road and onto the low wooden porch of the building. Through the open door the sounds of clinking cups and harsh laughter spilled out, and the accents of a dozen languages could be heard in the voices of the travelers within.

Varelia was not always the destination for those who arrived here in the hamlet. Most were merely traveling from one location to another and their paths naturally bisected the foothills of the small kingdom. As a settlement erected primarily for the benefit of the Varelian nobility passing in and out of the mountain realm, it was a well-built, well-stocked resting place for many a discerning drifter. And that meant that the tavern was always filled with representatives of various cultures.

A moment after entering the large common room the voices fell silent. The creaking of leather and muttered whispers were all that greeted the

Hunter as he stepped in off the porch. It was something he had grown accustomed to in his years of service to King Telarius. The mask and the helm always seemed to silence even the most inebriated and unruly of men.

He passed between the small round tables with slow steps and approached the bar where a man with a panicked expression and long mustache stood frozen. The Hunter placed his hand on the edge of the wooden counter and stared at the man for a moment. He then reached into his dark cloak and pulled out a small piece of paper, which he placed on the polished surface. Then, reaching again into his cloak, he produced a small cloth pouch that clinked softly with the sound of the coins inside when he placed it on top of the scrap of parchment.

The frightened bartender stepped forward nervously and slowly took the note and the pouch. After retreating a comfortable distance, he read the note and then disappeared through a door behind the bar. In the silence of the common room it was easy to hear the bartender rummaging through boxes and moving heavy objects. After a brief absence he reappeared with a leather pack, flat and large, that was filled to the brim and fastened at the top with two iron buckles.

"Th-th-thank you, Master," the man muttered, who then set the pack on the counter and withdrew again into the storeroom without turning away or lifting his bowed head. The Hunter lifted the bag, turned on his heels and then walked toward the door and the road beyond, leaving only the sounds of his boot steps as a reminder that he had been there.

Outside, Anthus awaited exactly where he had been left, and did not move even when he saw his master approaching. The Hunter carried the leather pack over to his horse and lifted it to tie to the back of the saddle when he heard a shout from the road.

"Hunter!" called out a large man. He was dressed in worn and poorly fitted armor that struggled to cover his muscular form. "We have a quarrel to settle, you and I."

The Hunter set his pack on the porch beside Anthus and stepped into the road a pace. The stranger was enormous, perhaps half a head taller than he was, and considerably heavier. He carried a short sword with a wide blade in one hand, and a small buckler in the other. His posture was aggressive, and he held his arms outward as if inviting an attack.

"'Kill a Hunter, be a Hunter' they say. I reckon today I will find out if that is a legend or a law in these lands." The stranger smiled wildly.

It was true, of course, what the man said. The Hunter served the King for as long as he could carry out his master's orders while remaining undefeated in battle. Fail the King, or suffer defeat, and the mantle would pass to the victorious party. Because of this the life of a Hunter was overrun with frequent challenges from men too brave for their own good. But a Hunter rose to the position for a reason, and any challenger that was courageous, or crazed, enough to approach one would find himself hard-pressed to win.

The stranger stepped forward and began to swing his short blade in small, slow arcs. The Hunter stepped another pace from his horse and then stood still as the larger man approached. With a guttural shout the challenger dove at him, cutting a wide curve with his sword from right to left. And then the Hunter was gone.

He had not vanished, however much it may have appeared that way to his attacker. Rather, he had smoothly sidestepped the coming blow and maneuvered himself behind his opponent. The hulking man lurched around and slashed wildly again, this time from left to right. Again, the Hunter evaded him.

"Fight me, Hunter!" he growled in frustration. The challenger took a step back, clashed his sword against the shield and then charged at his target once more while the sharp echo still hung in the air.

This time, though, the Hunter chose to act. As the stranger slashed down wildly at his head, he stepped to the side and struck out. The only weapon he held was his gloved fist, but the blow caught the other man directly on the jaw, breaking it with an audible crack. The brute staggered backward and grabbed his face, but though the punch may have silenced him, it did not stop him.

The hulking attacker rushed forward again, but this time he moved faster and drove his sword forward more precisely. The Hunter was fast, but this time he was unable to move to safety. As the blade thrust toward his chest he managed to swing his forearm upward to parry the blade out of the way. Then, with a well-placed kick, he swept the stranger's forward leg from underneath him, sending him toppling to the hard stone roadway.

The challenger grunted as he hit the

ground, and then tried to roll over quickly. The Hunter, however, now had the clear advantage. In a blur of movement he leapt into the air and landed upon the large man's chest. Then, with a flick of his wrist a small, delicate blade appeared in his hand, which he proceeded to press against the exposed flesh of is attacker's throat.

"Yield," he hissed sharply. He had won the battle decisively, and was in the position to offer the man his life, something not many Hunters would ever consider an option.

Somehow, through bloody teeth and a broken jaw, the defeated stranger managed to spit, leaving a mess of pink saliva on the silver beard of the Hunter's mask. Only with the man's refusal clear did the Hunter end the fight, coldly and quickly.

When he stood to clean the blood off the small blade he noticed that the occupants of the tavern had emerged at some unknown moment to watch the challenge unfold. Now they drifted quietly back through the dark doorway, preferring the comfort of their drinks to the risk of angering the victorious Hunter. Alone, he walked back to the leather pack and to Anthus who had remained standing on the side of the road.

The Hunter cleaned his blade and returned it to the hiding place in which he kept it. Then, after tying the pack to the back of the saddle, he placed a boot in one of the stirrups and pulled himself up onto the horse. He took one last glance around the tiny hamlet, up toward the mountaintop palace and down at the man he had just killed, and then urged Anthus forward with a light kick of his heels.

As the pair stepped out into the valley, the dark forms of both rider and mount vanished into the fading light of dusk. The Hunter had always traveled best at night. And though the journey ahead was familiar enough, the small voice of experience was quick to remind him that the dead stranger on the road behind him would certainly not be his last challenge.

Chapter 7

Simon woke to the sound of rain beating down through the canopy of leaves above. The light was dim and grey and the air had grown thick with moisture. The fire from the night before still smoldered near his feet, hissing occasionally as drops of water slipped through the trees and landed on the glowing red embers.

It took Simon a moment to realize Sir Lovelace was gone. Billy the horse was still tethered to a tree nearby, but his owner was not present. Simon stood and stretched his stiff limbs, and then pulled an apple from the pack on the ground near the horse. He took a large bite for himself before holding the rest out for Billy to eat. The apple quickly disappeared, replaced by a muffled crunching sound.

Taking a look around the camp, he noticed that they had settled in a small clearing with a meager layer of moss and short grass on the ground. It had been too dark to see the evening before when they finally returned with the firewood, though Simon had wondered why the ground felt so soft as he slipped easily into the sweet arms of sleep.

"Simon, lad," came a familiar voice from behind him. He turned to see Sir Lovelace stepping back into the camp, a brace of squirrels strung from his belt. "I trust you slept well enough?"

Simon nodded. "Has it been raining long, Sir Lovelace?"

"Montgomery," he replied, stepping toward the smoldering fire.

"Sir?" Simon was not sure what the knight meant.

"My name. Call me Montgomery. Or Sir Monty, if you must," he responded. "If we are to be traveling and adventuring into the wild unknown together, the least we can do is afford ourselves a small bit of familiarity and comfort. So if you please, you may address me as Sir Monty."

Simon relaxed with a smile. "Certainly, Sir Monty," he added.

The knight removed the results of his morning hunt from the cord on his belt, and began to prepare them for roasting. He pulled the dagger from his hip and expertly skinned and dressed the squirrels while Simon watched.

"They are not much to look at, I admit," he offered in consolation. "But they will help us feel human today. I hate beginning my day on an empty stomach. It seems unnatural. Now, be a good lad and try to find us some dry wood to add to the fire."

With a nod the young man stepped out of the camp and into the tangle of underbrush and tree trunks of the forest. The rain was slowing with the growing light, though it was still little more than a pale glow. Simon searched under shrubberies and inside the carcasses of fallen trees for any piece of dry kindling he could find, and eventually made his way back to camp with a small bundle tucked under one arm.

The fire leapt quickly to life under the attention of the experienced knight, and soon their meal was cooking over the flames. With a moment of respite and waiting before them, Simon decided he would attempt to learn more of the knight's objectives for this journey.

"Can I ask about the dragon, Sir Monty?" he asked hopefully. Talk of such things was never allowed by his parents – a word that he now used reluctantly out of a frustrated lack of better options — and was rarely discussed even among the other children of Bywood. They were a practical people, not given to fancy and folly and tales of the mysterious. But Simon was no longer in Bywood, and his view of the world was in need of growth and change.

"Ah yes, the dragon," Sir Monty replied pensively. "The Red Drake, he is called. To some he is known as the Bhen Thaire. I myself prefer to think of him as a large worm, though I have yet to see an actual worm that has the powerful legs and expansive wings that the Red Drake possesses."

The knight seemed subdued by his thoughts and stared into the glowing center of the fire. Simon waited in silence for what seemed to be an eternity before the man continued.

"He is ferocious, " Sir Monty continued, "and full of greed. And though countless warriors have tried, no one has yet managed to defeat him. His breath burns with fire and his teeth drip with poison. With talons sharper than diamonds and scales stronger than steel, he is the perfect monster, and though heroes have tried, all have failed."

Simon listened carefully and thought about the knight's words. "And your goal, you have said, is to be the one to do that? To defeat the Red Drake?"

The older man smiled and nodded, but his actions lacked as much confidence as one would have expected from someone so determined. "I have already failed once before, but I left my mark on the beast. I aim to return and finish that which I have begun."

He glanced at the fire, and almost immediately hopped up. "Our meal appears to be done," he declared. "Come, lad, let us break our fast and begin the day's journey toward adventure!"

As the morning pushed on toward early afternoon, the rain vanished, and with it the warm, humid air. A cool breeze was blowing in from the north, cutting between the countless tree trunks to bite at Simon's hands and face. He was glad to have brought a warmer change of clothing and used a momentary pause in their journey to quickly pull the extra garments on.

With the cool air came the fog, as dense as smoke. The light of the day seemed to be choked off by the white fingers that swirled around the trees and through the branches. Along with the subdued light, the sounds of the ancient forest had been muffled, casting an eerie stillness on their path. But Sir Lovelace was confident of the direction they needed to travel, and so he pressed on, though their steps were more cautious now.

Simon felt as if their blind walk through the forest would never come to an end. Without something ahead to set his gaze upon, it was difficult to determine whether they were making progress, or if they had somehow walked in one large, continuous circle without realizing it. He was about to ask Sir Lovelace if he truly knew the way through the fog, when he saw a dark shape out of the corner of his eye.

The fog had mingled in and around the trees, but their thick trunks were still partially visible in the small area around their path. But trees were not meant to move, and when Simon caught another glimpse of something moving, he held his breath and tapped the knight on his shoulder.

He wondered to himself if it was the mysterious woman he met the day before. She claimed to be a wood nymph and called herself Juno, though until now Simon had doubted he had really spoken to her. But here, in the mist and dense forest, perhaps his dreams had drifted closer to the waking hours than he had expected.

"I see it too, lad," whispered Sir Lovelace without turning to face him. "It has been there for some moments, but it appears to be keeping its distance. I shall have to assume that whoever or whatever it is, that it is unaware that we are here."

The knight guided Billy to a stop and then waited in silence for a moment. Then, with a hand cupped around his mouth, Sir Lovelace hailed the unknown presence.

"Ho, there!" he shouted. Though he attempted to be as loud as possible, his voice was muffled by the fog. The figure ahead of them stopped, and for a brief moment it blended in amongst the dark forms of the trees. And then something unexpected began to happen.

The shape moved toward them.

At first it was difficult to discern whether the shape was moving at all, so blurred was their view by the heavy mists. But occasionally the path between them was impeded by a large tree, and Simon could see the dark form step around it. Moments passed before even a footstep could be heard. And then the mists appeared to part and a figure came into view.

It was a woman, old and stooped, with a weathered face and gnarled fingers. She wore a long, plain skirt of brown wool which hid her feet from view. Around her shoulders she had drawn a thin shawl tight against the cold. Her nose was bent, her eyebrows were thick and on the whole she reminded Simon of Mrs. Blackstone, the wife of the elderly man who owned the general store in Bywood.

"Quit y'er shoutin', young man," she whispered harshly at the knight. "You'll frighten 'way all the spirits. An' the spirits are what I'm chasing." She glanced around the forest as if looking for something.

"You are looking for spirits?" asked Simon curiously. The old woman turned and stared at him, and her bright green eyes seemed to cut right into him.

"No, lad," she said curtly. "I know where they are. The trouble is catchin' 'em."

She held up a small egg-shaped basket of tiny, woven twigs. It was oddly shaped for a basket, with a rounded top and a small opening which the woman had plugged with a wad of damp cloth. "Them spirits are terribly difficult t' get my hands on, but when I do I take no chances. Into the rowan basket they go. I keep 'em inside with this rag doused in vinegar and rapeseed oil. Smells horrible, but it works well enough."

"Who are you, woman?" Sir Lovelace asked with a skeptical tone. "And cease with the talk of spirits. You're making my companion uneasy."

Simon balked at the suggestion but did not respond to the comment. Instead, he pressed further with the woman. "Why do you wish to catch these spirits?"

"Ah, yes," she sighed satisfactorily, "that would be the better question, would it not? Why is the old hag prancing 'round the Aldwode searchin' for wisps and spirits? Because, young man, the spirits tell me things."

"They what?" he asked with a growing curiosity. "The spirits talk to you? What do you speak to them about?"

The old woman laughed and the sound of it drove chills down Simon's backbone. "The spirits an' I do not converse in the same manner you an' I are speakin' right now. No, the spirits do little listenin', truth be told. They speak t'me. They speak at me, as it were. Tell me things, they do."

"Simon, lad," interrupted Sir Lovelace, "you are encouraging this woman's madness and delusion. Let us continue on our way."

Simon ignored the knight, though, and climbed down off the horse. "What do they tell you?"

The woman paused and looked carefully at him for a moment, appearing to consider the question before answering. Then she extended the small basket toward him and nodded at it.

"These spirits tell me 'bout the future," she whispered. "I'll ask 'em 'bout yours if yer wantin' me to."

"I don't think that would be a wise..." Sir Lovelace attempted to stop the conversation, but Simon was enthralled by the mysterious woman. She was unlike any of the regular travelers who had passed through Bywood in the past. Simon found this intruiging, especially now that he had left his home, and all that it entailed, behind him.

"Tell me, please," he requested eagerly.

The old woman looked about herself again, and then reached down to the basket and removed the wet rag. She stared into the black hole for a moment, and then she began to chant. Her voice was muffled by the thick fog around them, and she kept her voice low and deep. But the words were uttered with a mesmerizing rhythm, and Simon could not help but listen closely.

Slowly, as her words beat out like the tapping of a large, guttural drum, a wisp of pale mist drifted out of the basket's small opening. It moved like smoke yet there was no odor, and it shimmered with a soft light of its own. Like the tip of a vine, the vapor inched upward, toward the old woman's head. And then her chanting stopped.

Sir Lovelace shifted uneasily in the saddle as he watched the woman and the mist from on top of the horse. Then, after a brief pause, the strange woman inhaled sharply. The smokey wisp slipped between her weathered lips and vanished into her mouth. And as it did so, her eyes closed and she slumped forward, completely still and silent.

Simon began to worry for the woman. He could not hear her breathing and she was not moving. Yet she stood before them, holding the unstopped basket, like a statue. And then she lifted her eyes and took a long, deep breath before setting her gaze upon the young man.

"Lost..." she hissed at him. "You are lost...far from where you belong...but you will find your true source..."

She swayed as she spoke, and Simon noticed that even though she was facing him, her eyes were not entirely focused on his. It was as if she were speaking to someone else.

"Others will help you...many dangers...but you must stay true to your destiny...hold true to the quest," she whispered hoarsely, the rough voice coming from deep within her. "Trust will be your light...beware the deceivers and liars...look to the forest..."

Sir Lovelace shifted uncomfortably in the saddle. "This is nonsense, lad. It means nothing, can you not tell?"

"A hunter," she hissed louder. "You will face a hunter of men...you will bring defeat upon the hunter...he will be shown for who he really is..."

The woman coughed suddenly, nearly dropping the basket. She shook her head and closed her eyes again, bending forward as if in pain. And then the mist reappeared, issuing forth from her open mouth before drifting lower and vanishing back into the basket.

"What did all of that mean?" Simon asked her expectantly. "What hunter will I face? What is my true destiny?" He felt as though the spirit offered little by way of answers, managing instead to create more confusion for him.

The old woman shook her head. "I d'not know what the spirits know, lad. But mark my words, if it is a Hunter you shall face, then you best be careful. Hunters are not to be trifled with."

"That may be the first sensible statement she has uttered, lad," Sir Lovelace said.

Simon swallowed hard. "But," he stammered weakly, "you said I would defeat him somehow."

"Did I, now?" The woman's eyes lit up, and she stepped closer to the young man. "Well then, lad, you may be able to offer me a suitable payment for my services, if you d'not mind me askin' of it." She smiled wryly at him.

"Payment?" exclaimed Sir Lovelace. "Payment for that farce of a performance? You never warned the lad you would require anything in return, you miserable hag. Take your motley bag of tricks elsewhere, O Queen of the Ghosts."

The woman shot a fiercely cold look at the knight and then leaned toward Simon and bent closer to his face. "The Hunter's soul is all I ask for. Nothing of value t'you, of course, lad. Just the soul of the one you shall defeat. I will be there to claim it upon your victory. The Hunter's soul."

"Simon," the knight interjected briskly, "it is time we take our leave." He reached down and gripped the young man's shoulder and Simon nodded. Even Billy the horse was anxious to be moving on, his tail swishing erratically. "Begone, hag."

The old woman stepped back reluctantly as Simon was helped back up onto the horse behind the knight's saddle. He did not fully understand what the woman had told him, but he had heard enough that he now felt worrisome about his future. He wanted more than anything to stay and discover as many answers as he could, but if Sir Lovelace did not trust the strange woman then perhaps he should not either.

As the knight guided them away down the foggy path, Simon glanced back at the old woman, who stood where they left her. She stood as still as one of the countless trees, and as the fog closed in around her it was no longer possible to tell her apart from the rest of the shapes of the ancient forest. Whatever truths lay behind them were now lost in the mists. Simon's only hope for answers lay ahead.

Chapter 8

The map led the Hunter south down the old High Road to the fringes of the Aldwode, the most ancient of woodlands. It was a long journey down from the foothills of the Ironbrood mountains, taking nearly a day on horseback. But the Hunter rarely slept and therefore rode through the night, arriving near his destination as the first rays of the sun were climbing over the hills to the east.

As the High Road brought him to the edges of the forest it connected with another road that ran from the east to the west, winding a path along the borders of the wooded expanse before vanishing over the horizon. His journey did not lay in either direction, however, and he brought Anthus to a slow stop at the turn in the road.

A chill morning air was blowing down from the north pressing the Hunter's cloak tight around him from behind. His horse remained as still as stone, with not even a twitch of the tail to signal displeasure at the cold wind. Only the sound of the trees could be heard, like a soft whisper above them.

The Hunter led Anthus off the security of the paved roadway that had served them well so far, and continued their path southward into the low grasses and shrubs that lined the road. The ground was uneven, but his experienced eyes could see the traces of a path. Though not used regularly, it appeared to have been used frequently enough to point him in an obvious direction. Tucking the map back into his cloak, he urged Anthus farther along and trusted his eyes.

Though the sky above glowed with the pale dawn light, the forest before him was shrouded in darkness and seemed to remain in eternal night. The tree tops high above were clothed in a thick canopy of subdued greens and browns, but the world between their wide trunks was one of shadows. Stepping into the forest felt like entering a house, with close walls and muffled sounds. No matter how many times he had travelled here, the Hunter could not help but feel as though he were trespassing.

Away from the cover of the grasses and shrubs, the path became more apparent. A worn trail weaved between the cramped tree trunks and led out of sight into the dim light. The Hunter followed the path slowly, ducking under low branches and easing Anthus through the confining spaces.

After another hour the pair suddenly stepped into a sparse area with fewer trees than they were used to. The tenuous branches above seemed to let in more light as well, illuminating the small grove with a soft yellow glow. The farther they travelled, the wider the spacing between the trunks became, until suddenly they stood at the edge of a large clearing.

Light spilled out of the clearing into the darker forest beyond and it took a short moment for the Hunter's eyes to adjust. And then he saw it. Sitting in the center of the open space, under the bright light of the morning sun, was a large, sprawling homestead.

It was a low structure, crafted of large timbers and covered with a neatly thatched roof. A tall fence had been erected around the house, extending out and encompassing a large portion of the open clearing. The far end of the fence connected with a second building, much larger than the first, with massive doors that stood wide open. It was a barn.

Cautiously, the Hunter urged Anthus forward across the short grass of the bright glade. As he approached the dwelling he could see a small group of horses standing near the large barn. They were noble creatures, beautifully tended and well cared for compared to many of the horses that he had encountered over the years. They looked, in fact, to be royal horses, such was their grace and manner.

"You there," came a voice from behind. The Hunter turned to see a man approaching from the direction of the dwelling. His features were sharp and strong, and though his hair was flecked with grey, he appeared to be full of youth. It was his eyes, however, that spoke of his true age.

"May I be of assistance to you?" the stranger asked in a deep tone. The Hunter dismounted and stepped toward the man, extending his hand in greeting. "Ah," he said, "you are a Hunter. I see."

The Hunter nodded. He knew he would have to speak more frequently than he was accustomed to, and searched for the correct tone to take. There was information he needed in order to accomplish his mission, and this man was a potential source. He needed to be cautious and respectful.

"I have traveled from Varelia in the north in search of someone of importance," he said as he stepped closer. "I am inclined to believe that you are that someone."

The stranger appeared to consider the Hunter's words for a moment. He cast an observant glance toward the great black steed who stood silently and obediently behind his master, and then shook the Hunter's gloved hand before motioning toward the stables. "I am Perian," he said calmly, if not anxiously, "let us walk together for a moment."

They approached the fenced area connected to the stables where the group of horses was gathered in the sunlight. Perian rested his arms on the fence and placed one of his boots on the lower crossbeam. The Hunter stood beside him, straight and tall and clothed in black amidst the green and sunlight of the wide clearing, and waited in silence for his host to speak.

Long moments passed before the man named Perian spoke again. When he did, he began with a question.

"You seek to learn of Toren, First King and

Lord of the Ironbrood Mountains, correct?" His voice sounded both exhausted and relieved to speak the words.

The Hunter nodded, confirming the man's suspicions. Then, more silence. After a much longer pause than the first, Perian began his tale.

"Long ago, before these lands were filled with men and roads and towns, there was only the Iron King. The King travelled far from his homeland in the white, cold North and crossed the mountains to enter this fine country. It was warm and bountiful, and with great skill and care the King tamed the wildness of the land and filled it with wonders of his own making.

"King Toren set himself first to building a magnificent palace high atop the mountains, looking down upon the new lands that he would rule. And soon others came. Like a moth to a flame, they were drawn to the power and glory that the Iron King wielded. And the source of that power was the magic crown upon his brow.

"The crown was forged by Velentar, the very god of forges and blacksmiths the world over, and in the forging it had been woven and folded with magic such as no wizard or witch had ever known. The crown was a gift to Toren, though the legends falsely accuse him of theft and trickery. And from that crown the King drew the power needed to conquer this land for himself, and to set up a just and noble rule over those who settled here.

"Centuries passed, for the Men of the North lived longer lives than those of the South, and the magic of the crown extended even that beyond its normal limits. And after a long, full life, the Iron King surveyed his kingdom. He had brought all of the lands south of the mountains under his reign, sired seven sons and seven daughters, and brought peace to the borders where war had waged as long as memories could recall.

"And so it was that Toren abdicated the throne to his oldest son, Lugus, and set out on a journey to preserve the peace he had crafted for future generations. Gathering those closest advisors and champions that he held dear, the King descended the mountain and made his way south to hide his magical crown away from those who might seek to use it's power for evil. A great expedition was mounted, with Toren traveling in his coach, drawn by twelve of his finest horses and guarded by six of his most decorated and accomplished knights. Countless servants travelled with the party, including a royal cook, the stable master and a court astronomer.

"The King and his companions then traveled south along the High Road until their path took them into the Aldwode, ancient then even as it is today. But after many hours of arduous travel through the thickly wooded paths of this forest, Toren decided it would be best to leave all but the most essential companions here with his coach while he and his knights continued their journey."

Perian motioned toward the barn and horses set before them. "This encampment that you see is what became of those who remained behind. The stable master was in fact my ancestor and forefather. And each generation has passed down what it knows to the next; the care of the royal horses, the true telling of the final journey of King Toren and the goal of that expedition. I serve today, as my father and all the generations before him also served, as a signpost pointing the way to the final destination of that fateful journey."

The Hunter considered this information for a moment. "And you have told many others what you have now told me?"

"No," Perian replied. "You, as it happens, are the first to have made it this far. Others have tried, of course. They have traveled through the dense paths of the Aldwode in search of answers. Many have even entered this very clearing and spoken with the keepers who came before me. But none have proven themselves worthy to know the truth."

"What then has set me apart from the others who have sought that which I too seek?"

Perian considered the question carefully for a moment before responding. "You, O Hunter, are the first to pass through this forest on a steed as mighty, well-trained and intelligent as those who served Toren himself. Only one who values such loyalty and strength is worthy to continue the journey."

The Hunter had begun to feel hopeful. His Master's desire to find the crown had seemed nearly impossible only a day before, but Perian had given him a small seed of hope. However, he knew that his journey had just begun, and that there was still much to be discovered. He needed to acquire any available clue to ensure his success.

"What can you tell me of the Iron King's journey from this location after separating from those who remained behind?" he asked openly.

"Ah," Perian replied, "it may seem as

though my knowledge would end here in this clearing, I know. And I cannot fault you for failing to trust me completely yet. But it is important to add that my ancestor followed the King beyond these wooded hills and to the end of his journey before returning to care for the remaining horses."

Perian produced an apple from one of his pockets and held it out toward one of the closest mares. The horse slowly approached the fence, and after smelling her master's hand, she took the apple between her jaws and quickly trotted away to join the others.

"Not all of the King's expedition can be shared. Some pieces simply must be discovered on your own. What I can tell you, though, is that the King and his knights traveled southwest from this location, to the area of the Aldwode where the Hesperus exits the forest before flowing into the west. It was there that the King and his champions made camp before the next stage of their journey."

The Hunter stepped back from the fence and extended his hand to Perian. "Then that is the destination to which I must travel," he declared decisively. "I thank you for your trust, and for your assistance."

A short whistle summoned Anthus, and the

Hunter expertly caught the horse's neck and swung himself up into the saddle. He turned to ride back into the forest, and as he departed Perian offered him a valediction.

"May your steed be swift," he called after him, "and may your travels be safe. Farewell!"

Chapter 9

"We have made good time, lad," said the knight cheerfully, looking up at the small blue opening in the treetops above them.

Simon was glad to hear they were making progress. He had expected the forest to thin once they crossed the River Estin, the waterway that separated the Aldwode from the Drakewood. But they had found the trees on this side of the river to be just as dense and confining as those they had left behind. The only difference, it seemed, was that the thick undergrowth they had grown accustomed to had been replaced with a gritty soil held together with loose clumps of weeds.

They had traveled three full days from Bywood, and this, the morning of their fourth, had proved to be their most productive yet. After walking for seemingly endless hours through the densely wooded hills of the Drakewood the trees began to thin. Here and there a fragment of sky broke through the dark canopy, as if a giant slate had fallen off the roof of the woodland. The patches of light became more frequent, and soon the pair found themselves passing in and out of small clearings where the underbrush gave way to bare earth and black, glassy rock.

"We are drawing closer," Sir Lovelace commented, pointing to the stones around them. The black rock looked odd and unnatural, with ripples and round edges. "This is dragon-melt, the warped and withered remains of scorched earth."

Simon stepped carefully around the small outcroppings of dark rock as if they were still molten and deadly, though he knew that not to be the case. The knight took the opportunity to dismount and lead Billy along behind him.

"We will have an easier path on foot from here onward," he said, making his way across the clearing. "Billy is a good horse, but he will soon begin to resist my guidance as his natural instinct takes over. Dragons, you see, love to eat horses."

Simon swallowed hard.

The next clearing was larger, and the opening in the treetops above offered a view unlike any Simon had seen before. Through the gap in the branches it was easy to glimpse the peak of a lone mountain, tall and steep, jutting from the forest ahead of them. It was a jagged spire of barren rock, charred and smoking, that rose high into the sky.

It reminded Simon of a chimney, but one that had been allowed to fall into disrepair and crumble about itself. The peak seemed to touch the sky and spray forth with a thin ribbon of dark smoke. Something burned within the mountain, though whether it was a furnace or the dragon himself Simon did not know. What he had no difficulty understanding, however, was that he was about to place himself in grave danger.

"Behold the lair of the great worm himself, lad," came the voice of Sir Lovelace from behind him. The older man had shown himself to have a flare for the dramatic, but this comment still caused Simon to pause for a moment. Few children from his village would have dared to dream of a real dragon's lair, and yet here Simon was on the verge of actually entering one.

"How close are we, Sir Monty?" Simon asked as he turned back to the knight. Sir Lovelace was holding his dagger in one hand and looked out of sorts, the proximity to their goal no doubt beginning to wear away at his nerves. Simon wondered what events transpired in that gnarled, smoldering lair the previous time the knight had traveled through these woods.

The knight stammered for a moment. "N-n-not far," he managed. Then, sheathing his blade and reaching for Billy's reins, he stepped toward one of the nearest trees and tied them to a low branch. "We should quicken our pace, lad. The sun will not wait for us, and we will need all the light we can get if we are to reach the threshold of the lair safely."

"Lead the way," Simon replied with a nod, and then shifted his pack and fell in line behind the experienced knight.

Soon the last fringes of the Drakewood had fallen away behind them as they ascended the small foothills that clustered around the base of the solitary mountain. The sun, too, had chosen to remain behind, and the afternoon sky was a bright, cheerful contrast to the cold darkness of the black rock as they approached the mountain's western side.

At last they crested the final black hill and found themselves walking toward the wide expanse between two steep inclines that extended outward, roots of the very mountain itself. And there between the rock walls, carved out of the stone surface, was the entrance to the dragon's lair. Dark and wide, the cavernous opening was completely exposed, like the gaping mouth of a giant.

"You say you left your mark on this beast?" Simon inquired as they continued through the path toward the entrance. "What did you mean?"

The knight did not turn his way, but kept his eyes on the dark opening ahead. "I wounded the great worm," he replied softly, as if he were afraid to alert the stones to their presence. "I challenged the Red Drake to battle, and made my stand. He was fierce and quick and full of hatred. But after much struggle I managed to wound him."

"Then what?" Simon was enthralled. To be speaking with one who had actually fought with a dragon was something he never expected. And yet here he was, traveling with the man, about to enter the lair of the same creature for another battle.

"Then I was forced from the lair," Sir Lovelace responded flatly. "The task was left unfinished. But today I plan to finish what I started."

They stopped at the threshold of the entryway and peered inside. Simon lifted his eyes to the opening itself and wondered at the incredible height of it, soaring perhaps fifty paces above them. He also noticed how smooth the edges of the entrance were, as if the dragon's body had rubbed against the stone as it passed, polishing the stone and removing the roughness over centuries of use.

"Should I light a torch, Sir Monty?" he asked, looking again into the darkness of the tunnel.

The knight shook his head. "No, lad. That would be akin to shouting our arrival into the bowels of the mountain. We will do well to maintain the element of surprise. But do not fear the darkness, for this foul beast is easy to find if you know where to look."

Sir Lovelace gave Simon a knowing wink and then stepped inside. Simon quickly followed, not wanting to become separated from his experienced companion at such a critical moment. Once inside, the atmosphere immediately felt different, as if the seasons had changed in an instant. The cool breeze of the mountainside had been replaced with a warm, humid air that hung heavy around them, and Simon could feel a low, steady rumble through the soles of his boots.

The sunlight reached into the cavernous tunnel a dozen paces or more, and by the dim light

Simon could see bones piled against the far edges. Some still lay on the floor nearby and he had to step carefully over them so as not to make noise and alert the dragon to their presence. While maneuvering over one particular heap he glanced down to see that it was a nearly intact skeleton, still clad in the rusted armor that failed to protect it.

Their footsteps fell almost silently on the stone floor thanks to a thin layer of dust and soil that lined the passageway. Simon stayed abreast with Sir Lovelace for fear of losing him in the growing darkness, but also kept enough distance between them so as not to appear weak or needy. But as the light faded behind them a constant low, rhythmic hum was beginning to fill the air ahead.

Simon turned to ask the knight about the sounds but the older man held a lone finger up against his lips to keep him quiet. Instead, he nodded his head toward the depths of the tunnel, and slowly Simon began to see what Sir Lovelace was heading toward. There, off in the indeterminable distance, a faint red glow pulsed like the beating of a heart.

It was the dragon's lair. With every pulsation of red light the guttural vibration grew louder, and then both faded for a moment.

Suddenly it occurred to Simon that he was hearing the breathing of the great beast itself. The dragon lay ahead, possibly sleeping, and they were moving directly toward it. Simon's legs felt weak and numb but he pushed himself to continue.

And then they arrived. At the end of the massive tunnel the space opened up even more into a vast cavern filled with red light. The ceiling was so high above them that Simon could only see darkness when he looked up. As they huddled together behind a large boulder resting against the edge of the entryway, they peered into the crimson lair and set their eyes on its occupant.

The Red Drake lay at the back of the cave, his head resting on the floor facing the entrance. He was incredibly large, larger than any animal Simon had ever seen, and true to his name he was clad in shimmering crimson scales as large as shields. Running along his back and neck were a series of large protrusions, like blades, that extended all the way down his long tail.

His head was larger than Billy the horse, long and narrow with a prominent chin and sharp brows. As the creature slowly breathed, its mouth opened revealing a set of vicious teeth that gleamed white against the red lips. Most surprising of all, however, was the fact that the dragon's glowing yellow eyes, large and round, were open and looking straight at them.

"Show yourselves, for I know you are there," the voice rumbled across the floor like a rolling boulder. "I caught your scent the moment you stepped onto my mountain, though I would rather you had brought the horse with you. It has been so long since I have had a proper meal."

The creature drew his legs beneath himself and then lifted his head off the ground. Metal rattled around him and Simon could make out the shine of gold and silver scattered all across the cavern floor. Though he knew very little about dragons he was positive that they loved treasure, and typically had a hoard that they curated and protected.

"Well?" the beast growled again, stepping toward them. "Come out where I can see you."

The Red Drake took slow, deliberate steps toward them, his massive limbs helping drive him forward across the treasure-strewn floor. His feet were enormous and tipped with razor-sharp talons that scratched at the stone like metal blades. Simon could not take his eyes off of the beast, and watched as it came nearer to their hiding place.

And then he noticed the limp.

The dragon moved slowly because he was favoring his hind left leg. It was not clear why, but the creature put little weight on that foot and shifted quickly back to the other leg for support. Moving this way, the dragon made his way slowly across the cave to within a few paces of the entrance where they hid.

Suddenly Sir Lovelace stood and revealed himself, placing a hand on Simon's head and holding him down while drawing his sword with the other. Peering from around the stone, Simon could see the dragon's face twist in surprise.

"You!" the dragon growled. Whatever the source of the red glow in the cave, the light had flared brighter as he spoke. "So you have finally returned to allow me the chance to finish what I began?"

Sir Lovelace laughed sharply at the enormous beast and waved his sword in the air. "I believe you are mistaken, you foul worm," he spat back. The knight then stepped from behind the boulder, moving out into the openness of the entryway fully exposed. "I have returned to complete my victory over you and claim your treasure. Our last encounter only proved to me how weak and helpless you truly are."

Taunted, the great red beast rose up on his hind legs and lifted his head in a horrific roar that shook the very stone foundations of the mountain. Simon quivered in a heap behind the boulder as fire ignited within the dragon's mouth. And then, with the sound of a rushing river, the beast expelled a monstrous plume of flames in their direction.

At the sight of the flames, Sir Lovelace did something Simon never thought he would have believed had he not witnessed it with his own eyes. The knight, exposed and undefended in the mouth of the tunnel, dropped his sword and ran as fast as he could manage back the way they had come. In an instant, Simon found himself alone with the dragon.

Chapter 10

The retreating knight's frantic footsteps were still echoing through the tunnel when the dragon's large head suddenly appeared beside the boulder, peering at Simon from only a few feet away. The abandoned young man swallowed hard, feeling his heart slip deep into the pit of his stomach, and then braced himself for the moment of death. But that moment never came.

"Who are you?" the dragon asked, his anger abated for the moment. "You were not with that thief the first time he visited my lair."

Simon did not know what to do or say; he had never spoken to a dragon before and did not know if there was a particular etiquette to follow when doing so. He inched backward slowly, but quickly bumped into the wall and could go no farther. He was apparently trapped.

And then the dragon's head vanished. For a moment the cavern was silent, and then Simon heard a sound, as if someone were wrestling with an opponent. Curious, he crawled on his hands and knees to peek around the curve of the boulder, only to find the dragon seated near by. The great beast was positioned much like a dog does to clean its belly, sitting back on his rump with its legs open, and was attempting to bite or nibble at something on his foot.

"What are you doing?" he asked before he knew the words were leaving his mouth.

The dragon looked up for a moment and then returned to the spot in question. "An old injury, nothing more," he replied with less growl than before. And then he added, "Nothing that will prevent me from eating you right now and spitting your bones out in a corner, though."

Simon ignored the threat and stepped closer to the dragon, trying to see what spot the creature was worrying with his snout. Then it occurred to him that it was the bottom of the dragon's foot that was causing the irritation – the very same foot that he had nursed upon standing.

"I saw you limping," he explained as he stepped even closer to the dragon's enormous foot. The claws looked deadly, and Simon could only imagine the damage they could do in a proper battle. "Can I take a look for you?"

The dragon paused thoughtfully, his monstrous yellow eyes fixed on Simon's face. Then, with a dip of his head and a flex of his shoulders, which Simon took to be a shrug, the great beast extended his injured foot toward the young man.

"For many years this wound has irritated me," said the Red Drake, "and though I manage to ignore it most days it is the walking that hurts me the most. But try as I might to look for the wound, I am unable to see that which pains me."

Simon stepped toward the incredibly large foot, extended out toward him as if the dragon had stopped mid-step. He slowly, carefully reached out and placed his hand on the creature's skin and was immediately struck by the warmth he felt. Though obviously covered in thick, impenetrable scales, the dragon radiated heat as though it burned with fire from within.

He inspected the foot slowly, working his way from the tips of the claws to the back of the heal but found nothing. It was only when Simon ducked underneath the massive foot that he found what he was looking for. Protruding from the center of the dragon's instep, embedded deep in the softer unprotected flesh, was a sword. When he reached out and gently touched the hilt the dragon flinched and growled deeply.

"Be careful, human," the beast snapped. "I have killed many a seasoned knight for causing me less pain. You would be best to mind your manners."

Simon stepped out from under the foot and stood before the Red Drake. "You have a weapon stuck in your foot," he said. "No wonder you cannot walk without great pain and difficulty. But I would be happy to remove it for you, if you would let me."

The dragon considered Simon's words. "You are a brave young human, I must say. What you are asking is no small thing, for the wound is deep and the flesh is greatly sore. Do it quickly, and with care."

Nodding, Simon stepped back to the massive foot and gently guided it down to rest on the stone floor. He placed one of his boot heels against the dragon's heel and carefully wrapped his hands around the grip of the sword. With one quick heave he pulled hard on the weapon and felt it slip free, sending him toppling onto his back. The deed was done.

The enormous beast had let loose a long, low growl as the sword was removed, and now had switched back to attempting to clean the wound without success. Simon pulled himself up off the floor and glanced at the sword he now held. It was a long blade of finely polished steel and still appeared as new as the day it was forged. The hilt consisted of a simple grip of tightly wrapped black leather and a dark iron pommel. The cross-guard was the most decorative element of the sword, crafted to resemble small vines or thorns that curved up and surrounded the first inch or so of the blade.

It felt heavy in his hand, though Simon had never actually held a sword before today, as there had never been a need in his simple village. Looking about, he set the blade on the floor near his pack, which he then picked up and hung over his shoulder.

"Where do you think you are going," boomed the rough voice of the Red Drake.

Simon froze. He had thought he might be able to slip out of the creature's lair unnoticed while it was distracted by the removal of the sword. But the dragon had quickly moved to its feet when the young man made an attempt to leave. Simon opened his mouth to speak, but the dragon interrupted him.

"Unfortunately I cannot let you leave," he growled, "until I have sufficiently rewarded you for your assistance."

Simon had braced for certain death, but the beast's words broke his concentration. "What?" he stammered awkwardly. "Reward? You mean you do not plan to kill me?"

"I do not. Not any longer, at least." The dragon smirked, if one could call it that, and Simon could not help but smile back.

"What is your name, young human?"

"Simon," he answered.

"Simon," began the dragon, "you are standing where few have journeyed before. But unlike them, you will walk from this place alive and well. But before you do so, I invite you to take a reward from my treasure. Anything at all."

The dragon turned toward one of the walls and expelled a fiery breath, igniting a small pile of debris. The new light illuminated the darkness, revealing the true size of the lair and the extent of the valuables that had been gathered within it. Light glinted off of large piles of coins and jewelry, and dozens of gilded hilts protruded from the sea of gold and silver. It was breathtaking.

Stepping closer to the treasure Simon

noticed that not everything was as valuable as it seemed. Mixed in among the gold coins and silver chains and gemstones were hundreds, perhaps thousands, of keys. Simple keys, keys encrusted with jewels, keys small and large. Everywhere Simon looked his eyes fell on keys. And then he remembered the warning that the wood nymph had passed on to him while passing through the Aldwode.

"There are few things beside keys and gold that dragons love," she had said. Recalling this, an idea occurred to him.

"Excuse me," he said. "You seem to have a great many keys in your treasure horde."

The dragon blinked. "I do," he said. "They are a passion of mine, whether ancient or new; foreign or local; dwarven or arcane. I doubt there is anyone who knows more about keys than I do, nor possesses as many different kinds. Do you mean to suggest that you are more interested in taking a key than some other more valuable piece of treasure as your reward?"

"No, not at all," Simon replied. Reaching inside his shirt, he pulled the weathered iron key out and held it up for the dragon to see. "It is just that I wondered what you might be able to tell me about this key."

The Red Drake leaned in close, lowering his head to position one of his large eyes beside the key. Simon could feel the heat radiating off of the beast's skin. After a moment of study, and even a few surprisingly delicate sniffs of the old key, the dragon stepped back.

"It smells very old," he began. "And you have to understand that I am a very old dragon. What I mean to say is that this key has seen more centuries than even I have."

"I assumed it was old," Simon replied, "but not that old. Very interesting. But do you know anything else about it? What of the engraving?"

"Ah," the dragon responded. "Destiny. The inscription is most interesting, indeed. I have seen another key like this, long ago, but it lacked this inscription. And while I have no guess as to the meaning behind the word itself, I can tell you that the script was crafted by a dwarven artisan. The entire key, in fact, is of dwarven nature. Of this I am certain."

"Dwarves?" Simon wondered aloud. "You mean that the dwarves made this key centuries ago? Why? For what purpose? And why was it given to me at birth?"

The dragon raised an eyebrow. "An heirloom, is it? Alas, I cannot tell you more. Each key is a lasting testimony to the craftsman who brought it into being, and speaks loudly of their work and culture. But of its purpose, each key is unfortunately silent."

Simon felt defeated. He had found himself in a position more fortunate than he could ever have imagined, here in the presence of a dragon. One that might hold answers to some of the questions he had regarding the mysterious key. And yet it appeared that he would be leaving with more questions than before. Rather than being closer to knowing the truth, Simon felt he had stepped farther from it.

"But I know who can answer these questions of yours," the dragon said, as if in response to Simon's doubt and despair. "I think it is clear that you must travel to see the dwarves. Who better to tell you what purpose that key might have served. And though none of the dwarves alive today are as old as myself, they are gifted with long lives, and might yet have some recollection as to the meaning behind the inscription."

Simon suddenly felt hopeful again. The trail had not run cold after all.

"Thank you," he said. Then, realizing that he no longer had the company of Sir Lovelace to guide and protect him, his head filled with fear and uncertainty. "Can I trouble you further and ask where one might find the dwarves?"

"Where?" the dragon quipped. "Where the dwarves are always found, of course; deep within the bones of the world. There are few dwarves left, something I might have played a role in, but those that remain are situated near the hot springs south from these woodlands. They have abandoned most of their magnificent underground cities to gather in the ancient halls of Fel'nagast, the oldest and most revered dwelling in their culture."

"South it is, then," Simon replied. "I am not sure how I will reach it, now that my travel companion has abandoned me here without a horse or protection. But if I am to find answers to my questions and discover who I truly am, then I must somehow travel south. Thank you again. You have been most accommodating."

Simon retrieved his pack and began to leave the lair, but the dragon stepped into his path and lowered his head to the young man's level.

"You did a brave and selfless thing, aiding me with my injury, and for that I owe you more than any trinket in my horde. At the very least you must be sure to take the sword with you. On the journey ahead you may find need of it."

"Of course," Simon replied, taking the blade and slipping it through one of the straps on his pack. The sword added weight to his burden, but it also lifted his spirits.

"And lastly, I wish to give you one last piece of assistance to you by offering to take you as far as the northern edges of the dwarven mountains."

Simon did not know what to say. The Red Drake was offering to let Simon ride upon his back like a horse, something that frightened and honored him all at the same time. But his options were extremely limited, and the thought of a lonely journey from the Drakewood to some unknown mountain in the southern lands was daunting.

"I do not know how to respond, to be honest," he managed to mutter.

"Think nothing of it. I shall have you to your destination within a matter of hours, and will be back before the morning sun rises. But we must leave now. What do you say, young human? Will you be the first to ride upon my back?"

Simon smiled before answering.

Destiny: A Fairy Tale

"Yes!"

Chapter 11

The Hunter peered through the thick foliage of the Aldwode from his hiding spot, studying the open field that separated him from the sprawling abbey. The branches were thick, brushing against the iron antlers on his helm, and the light was fading fast. Only when he was certain that the open space was untended did he step from the cover of the forest and make his way toward the courtyard at the center of the complex of buildings.

The abbey was pure in its simplicity of construction, almost plain in fact. A single tower rose from the center of the building, which lacked turrets and pinnacles of any kind. Even the windows were sparse, lacking division or decoration, and they seemed more like holes in the stone than functional openings. It was as if the building itself had renounced the world and withdrawn into sacred silence.

After nearly four days of continuous travel

through what seemed to be the thickest portion of the Aldwode, the austere structure was refreshing. The path from the stable master Perian's abode toward his destination was difficult to follow and complete with all manner of obstacle and complexity. Though Anthus stood as a paragon of agility and endurance, even he seemed eager to leave the confines of the forest. Unfortunately for him, he had to be left behind near the tree line, while the Hunter continued on foot.

He could hear the Hesperus flowing close by on the other side of the field. The first stars were beginning to push through the darkening sky and shadows had blended with the growing darkness, making it easier to remain inconspicuous. And ahead of him stood his destination, the tall statue that rose from the flat emptiness of the abbey's courtyard.

Few of the windows in the abbey glowed with lamplight, clearly a sign that the community within was close to slumber and rest. Fragments of singing fell from the high windows above, perhaps a restless monk finding comfort in his song. The Hunter, though, was focused on the statue ahead. It was the reason he had waited for nightfall.

He had seen the statue from a distance

when he arrived at the edge of the forest more than two hours ago. The fields were still buzzing with the abbey's residents finishing their workday, though, and rather than deciding to approach them as he had Perian, he chose to lay in wait until they had retreated within their walls. The reason for his delay was the statue of a solitary figure.

Even from the dense tangle of branches and leaves the Hunter was able to recognize the crown in the hand of the figure. The craftsmanship of the statue was not nearly as detailed and refined as he had grown accustomed to seeing in Varelia, but it was clearly shaped by an experienced hand. The figure was that of a man, tall and powerful, lifting a simple, almost rudimentary crown above his head with one arm.

The man was dressed in the robes of a king, and stood tall upon a large, rounded stone. The entire statue was set upon a flat, round base that appeared to be crafted from ancient iron plates. There were eight plates, in fact, dividing the round platform into equal segments, and on each plate a scene had been tooled in relief. The presentation, overall, was impressive and reason to pause and stare.

The Hunter stepped toward the statue

reverently, his eyes fixed on the figure above. In the growing darkness the shape of the statue stood out from the pale sky in a way that seemed to accent the crown, making it easier to see. It was almost magical.

A glance down presented the Hunter with one of the decorative iron plates on top of the base. On it the image of the abbey's central tower had been etched, and a simplistic crown had been added beneath it. The plate to the left showed a gathering around the abbey, with men and women holding some sort of ceremony. Other images covered the rest of the plates, surrounding the stone base of the statue.

The Hunter stepped up onto the metal platform and stood tall, reaching upward. Even for a man as tall as he, the crown was set quite high above the ground, and stretch as he might, he was unable to touch it. He reached within his cloak and slowly, carefully pulled a long blade from its scabbard and lifted it high. The point of the blade tapped against the crown, but rather than knock it lose it gave off a sharp scratching sound, like a knife being dragged across a wet-stone.

The crown was fake.

Suddenly the Hunter felt embarrassed for

allowing himself to believe that the legendary crown of Toren, the first Iron King, would have been left to weather the elements for centuries in plain sight of travelers. He had allowed his weariness to influence his actions, and he silently chastised himself for that. Humiliated and angry with himself, he stepped off the iron plate to the earth below.

In the silence of the dusk it was easy to hear the rattling sound. One of the plates had moved ever so slightly beneath his feet. Turning around he was not sure which plate it was, so he stooped to inspect the two closest iron panels. The engraving to the right was the departure scene, showing the long train of knights on horseback surrounding the king's coach. Beside it was the plate that showed the abbey tower with the crown resting below its feet.

Suddenly the rattling sound made sense; the crown was literally beneath the tower. The Hunter squatted beside the statue's base and felt along the seams of the metal covering for the lose plate. He searched with his fingers until he found the gap that was slightly wider than the others, and after retrieving a small knife he pried the iron panel up and lifted it as quietly as he could.

The Hunter carefully set the iron plate on the ground beside the platform and peered inside the opening, but it was darker than the coming nightfall. An almost imperceptible breeze pushed up from the passageway, but no sounds or movement accompanied it. He picked up a small stone and dropped it into the darkness, counting the seconds before the sound of impact.

The short span of time told him it was a manageable drop. Reaching into his cloak, the Hunter produced a small torch roughly the size of his forearm, as well as a tinderbox with flint and steel. After a silent prayer that the bottom was clear of debris he swung his legs over the edge and dropped inside, landing with an uneventful thud on a hard stone floor.

He listened for a moment before moving. Years of experience told him that not every danger had the courtesy to announce its presence, and so committing to observation and attentiveness was the best way to guarantee his safety. Only after he was certain that there were no sounds coming from above him or down the passageway did he strike the steel and flint, setting the small torch alight.

The torch bloomed like a flower, giving off the scent of metal and burnt resin. Instantly the walls were painted with flickering yellow light and black shadows. The chamber was actually a tunnel, roughly a head higher than the Hunter's antlered helm, and perhaps as wide as three grown men. With a flat wall behind him, it was easy to decide which way to go, and so the Hunter made his way slowly down the passageway toward the darkened reaches beyond.

No more than a dozen paces later the tunnel came to an end, emptying out into a wide, tall chamber. The room was bare of decoration or furnishings as one might expect in an abbey, but the low altar against the far wall seemed far less appropriate. It was carved out of a large block of black rock and fashioned to resemble a tall mountain. The Hunter immediately recognized it as the very mountain upon which Varelia was perched.

Stepping closer he noticed the smooth, flat top that had been crafted to hold something. A circle had been etched into the stone, showing the outline of an object, clearly marking the place where it belonged. But though he looked around and behind the altar, the Hunter was unable to find the crown, and in his urgency to find that which he sought before his small torch burned out, he lowered his guard.

The voice that interrupted him came from the doorway to the tunnel behind him, and though it was hushed and even in tone, it clearly held authority and power behind it.

"Who are you," the voice asked calmly, "and why have you trespassed into the most sacred of our spaces?"

The Hunter spun around quickly, drawing a dagger from his side and taking a defensive position. But he found himself staring at a lone monk in the threshold, clad in plain brown robes and cloaked in a large hood. Though the man was unarmed, he stood between the Hunter and the chamber's only exit, making it impossible to escape without a confrontation.

"I seek the crown," he said. "King Telarius has sent me to retrieve what is his."

The monk smiled knowingly from within his hood. "Like so many who have come before you, that which you seek cannot be found within these walls, I am afraid."

"Then where can I find it?" the Hunter asked.

"That, stranger, is a question I must defer to another." The monk extended an arm, motioning toward the doorway. "I am Brother Michael. Please, follow me. The Abbot will have the answers you seek. I will take you to him."

Without another word the monk turned and walked away, disappearing into the darkness of the passageway. The Hunter considered the possibility of an ambush for a brief moment before deciding that the holy man seemed to be honest and trustworthy. He took one last hopeful glance at the black altar before leaving the chamber to follow the man.

At the end of the hall, with the bright stars of the night clustered in a small circle above them, the monk expertly began scaling the wall, quickly ascending to the mouth of the passage. The Hunter approached the wall and ran his gloved fingers over the surface, noting the small indentations that his torch had failed to illuminate earlier. Without hesitation he began to climb.

Once back at the foot of the statue the Hunter helped Brother Michael replace the metal plate over the opening to the passageway. Then, following the lead of his silent guide, he headed toward the main entrance to the abbey's central tower.

Inside the ancient stone structure the

Hunter was led to a large room set deep in the center of the tower. The room was lit by a pair of large iron braziers that sat upon tall stands on opposite sides of the room. The monks of the abbey had added rose clippings to the fires, as evidenced by the aromatic scents that filled the chamber. Set against the back wall across from the room's entrance was a small stone chair that resembled a throne, and seated upon it was a cloaked man.

The Hunter was led to within a few paces of the seated figure before Brother Michael quietly exited the chamber. Alone with the man draped in dark brown and shadows, he began to speak, but was cut off by a hoarse, raspy voice.

"I am Father Ambrose, Abbot of this community" he announced. "I understand that you have questions about the crown. You must forgive me, stranger, if I do not stand or make light conversation. For I am too old and weak, and my eyesight has long ago abandoned me. But my brothers tell me that you are dressed as a Hunter of the King, and that you have been resourceful in your pursuit of the prize."

"Yes," the Hunter replied.

"Very well. Let us discuss the story of this

abbey, then. I believe that within this ancient tale you may find some piece of information that can serve you in your journey."

The old man pulled his deep hood from his head, revealing an aged, withered face crowned by wisps of snow white hair. The abbot's eyes were dark, as if a light had been extinguished, and deeply set. But it was clear from the lines etched along his mouth and brow that he was a man prone to laughter and contemplation.

"Long ago, beyond even the length of my days, the Iron King traveled to this place. He sought to remove his crown, the source of his great power, from the reach of his less worthy children, intending to hide it away until someone worthy of its power came to claim it for their own.

"The King brought his finest knights with him, and they settled beside this great river while the preparations were begun to craft the final resting place for the crown. But the work required to bring this about was slow and difficult, and required the help of many odd and distant accomplices, and so a temporary home was needed for the crown. The King's men therefore built the chamber that you yourself have now discovered, and placed the crown upon its dark altar to be guarded and kept safe until the hiding place was completed.

"In order to protect the crown while it rested here, a tower was built over the chamber, and then buildings around the tower. Centuries passed since that first stone was laid, and the structure evolved and changed until at last the monks came and filled its cold halls with their chants and prayers. I am the forth abbot to have shepherded the men of this abbey, and my rule has been long. Centuries have passed since the tower was built, but the tales of Toren dwell among us like a brother."

"But the crown disappeared," interrupted the Hunter. "Where did it go?"

"Patience, child," the abbot rasped in reply. "Our tradition tells us that after years of preparation the hiding place was finally completed, and the crown was removed from the chamber to be interred there. Where the hiding place or the crown reside, we do not know. We only know that these walls once served to protect it, and we honor that tradition by guarding the chamber that once held it."

"What of those who aided the King in crafting the final hiding place?" the Hunter asked.

"What do you know of them?"

The Abbot gently shook his head. "I am afraid I do not know much. It is said that the King's chief knight, a man named Hector, worked closely with Toren to communicate with a witch to bring together the tools necessary to hide the crown. Objects were needed, objects of great power and cunning craft, to build this resting place. And the witch was knowledgable about these things.

"It is said that she was gifted with an unusually long life by Toren himself, though whether she still survives I know not. But I do know more about Sir Hector, for he was tasked with guarding the secret of the hiding place. Some say it was the location he guarded, while others believe he protected some sacred relic, a map or clue, perhaps, that the King required to be kept safe. But Sir Hector and the witch have both passed from our memories and entered the realm of legends. And that is all we guard today, I am afraid: legends."

The Hunter stood silently for a moment, taking the abbot's words in and working through them in his mind. The crown was taken from here and hidden away from the world, and the only witnesses to its disappearance have likewise vanished into the mists of time. His quest, it would seem, had suddenly become much more difficult.

"Thank you, Abbot," he said. "You have been most generous to one caught trespassing on sacred ground. If I may, I will take my leave now and follow my quest elsewhere."

"Of course," the Abbot replied. "And may your journey lead you to that which you seek."

The Hunter turned and left the chamber, stepping into the hall where Brother Michael stood waiting for him. The monk silently fell in step beside him and guided him back out of the abbey and into the dark night air. The Hunter turned to thank the monk for his assistance before retuning to Anthus and the dark embrace of the Aldwode, but Brother Michael drew closer.

"Forgive me, please, for my impertinence, but I overheard your discussion with the Abbot, and I may have information that could be of assistance to you. To the east of here, farther up river toward the center of the forest, a woman is said to dwell. She has been there for a very long time, longer than any of us can remember, and some whisper that she is cursed with an unnaturally long life. I do not know if this woman is the witch the Abbot spoke of, but I cannot think of another who more closely fits that description."

The Hunter nodded in agreement and placed a hand upon the monk's shoulder. "Thank you, Brother Michael," he said in a hoarse voice through his silver mask, "You have given hope to a hopeless man. For that, I will be forever grateful."

And with that the Hunter turned and dashed off into the night.

Chapter 12

Having only a few days of horseback riding to recall for comparison, the resulting flight on the back of the enormous Red Drake was an exhilarating experience. Even in the quickly fading light of the approaching evening Simon could see the trees and streams and broken roads that painted the ground below like miniature versions of their true appearance. The Drakewood resembled a sea of green that rippled in the wind, gently breaking against the plains to the south.

The journey was swift and uneventful, but for the unnatural feeling of fear and excitement at being so high off the ground. The dragon kept his head extended far out in front of his body, and his wings beat the air with a slow, steady rhythm. Simon sat upon the great beast's spine between two large protrusions that resembled tiny mountains and held on tightly so as not to be buffeted off by the wind.

The Red Drake did not speak through the

entire course of the journey south, though Simon doubted that he would have been able to hear the creature speak over the sound of the air rushing by his ears. Instead he studied the features of the world below as the afternoon's light faded to evening, noting the rise of a small mountain range that ran from north to south. And it was perhaps midway along this stretch of ancient mountains that the dragon finally flew lower and came to a quick but gentle landing at the foot of a small hill.

"Thank you again, young human," the dragon growled kindly as Simon slipped off onto the firm ground. "You have rid me of an old wound, and for that I am grateful to have met you. I am not certain that I can yet consider my debt to you repaid. Should you ever require my assistance, you need only ask. It would be my honor to give you what you need."

"Thank you," Simon said with a smile, glad to have made a friend of a creature so ancient and powerful. "And thank you for not eating me," he replied with a grin.

The Red Drake laughed a rough, grinding laugh that shook the hillside, and then turned to face the way they had come. "I do hope you find what you are looking for," he said. "Discovering who we are is far more important than being who we are expected to be. May your quest bring you the answers you seek."

Simon waved and watched as the dragon leapt high into the air, as a cat might do when pouncing on a mouse, and then unfurled his wings and took flight. The dragon's form quickly vanished into the dimming evening sky, and Simon quickly felt alone. He turned around to take one last look at the path that lay before him and caught the faint shimmer of water toward the south, but he knew it was much too far to attempt at this late hour.

Finding a comfortable place to sit near a small stand of pines, he set his pack down and began to rummage through it for a fire starter and a small hunk of stale bread. After setting up his meager camp and finding the most comfortable place to lay down for the night, Simon pulled his blanket over his tired body and closed his eyes as the stars above blinked and twinkled like crystals on a black cloth.

The smell of food pulled Simon from his sleep at an early hour of the morning. Grey had replaced black in the sky behind the dark silhouettes of the mountains, and the stars were quietly fading into the distance above. But it was the smell of food that seemed to be the most startling change.

In his bleary-eyed state Simon briefly entertained the notion that Sir Lovelace had returned and was preparing the food for the long day of traveling that lay ahead. But tossing aside his blanket and rolling toward the scent he quickly saw the fire that had been lit, and the small, lithe figure who sat beside it.

"And a good morning to you," called out a soft, feminine voice. Simon was suddenly fully awake and alert, and for a moment unsure as to who it was seated just a few steps away beside the fire. And then he remembered who she was.

"Juno," he said. "What are you doing here?"

"Cooking you something to break your fast, of course," she replied with a smile.

"No," Simon said, pulling on his boots and standing up, "that is plain to see. What I meant was, why are you here, in my camp, so far from the Aldwode?"

The young woman smiled, and for a moment Simon could not tell which was a warmer sight, the fire or Juno. And then, with a tone that was both calm and strong, "I have come to give you aid. You have stepped into a world that is vastly different from what you know, and have lost your companion and guide. I have come to help."

Simon pulled his blanket around his shoulders to fend off the chill of the early morning air, and then stepped over to take a seat beside the mysterious woman and her campfire. A small iron pan had been set above the flames, and strips of meat were sizzling inside it, giving off a scent that made his stomach rumble.

"But how did you find me?" he asked.

"I did not," she said. "Well, that's not true. I have simply followed you ever since we met, so I suppose I found you days ago, though I have stayed hidden and out of your path."

"Followed me?" Simon gasped. "Why?"

"Because I did not trust that the one you were traveling with would remain faithful to you. When I saw him run from the dragon's lair I feared that you had been killed, but imagine my relief when I saw you emerge from the cave unharmed. It took me all night to catch up to you after you flew away."

Simon was less surprised than he expected himself to be. Since leaving Bywood he had meet a wood nymph, had his fortune told to him by an old woman in the Aldwode, and made friends with a dragon. To find Juno sitting beside him now seemed less out of the ordinary than it probably should.

"Do you know where I am headed, then?" he asked after a moment.

"South," she replied confidently. "Most likely to the dwarves. There is little else worth visiting in this part of the world. If I can ask, what are you seeking?"

Simon stared at the flames for a moment before answering. Then, pulling the key out from his shirt, he held it up to the young woman. "I need to know where this came from."

"Ah yes," she replied. "Your key. I see you made it out of the dragon's lair with it still in your possession. Did you learn something about it from the Drake?"

"Yes," Simon said. "He tells me it is unmistakably Dwarven. So I am off to Fel'nagast to ask the dwarves if they can tell me when it was made, and for what purpose."

Juno stood. Simon noticed how the morning light played upon her auburn hair, making it seem as though it were on fire. She took the pan off of the makeshift rack above the flames and set it between them. Then, with a wave of her hand, she extinguished the fire in an instant.

"How did you..." he began to ask, but she interrupted him.

"Here, take some food. You will need your strength today. Fel'nagast is a long journey from here, and will take us more than a day."

She fell silent while Simon blew on the meat to cool it before taking a bite. Then, she slowly began her explanation.

"Remember, Simon, that I am a nymph. I am not immortal, but nor do I walk through the world with the same eyes as you. And as such, I have certain abilities that others do not. I have power over many of the elements, and can hear voices you do not know are there."

"But why are you following me?" he asked between mouthfuls.

"Because I was asked to," she replied. "Many years ago a man passed through our grove. He asked if we knew of the small village to our south, and when we confirmed that we did, he begged us to guard it. One day, he told us, a young man may venture out from its superstitious borders, and he pleaded with us for his protection."

"That could be me!" Simon realized. "Where did he go? What did he tell you about my key?" He shot questions at the woman like a hunter trying to bring down a stag.

"Please," she interjected, holding up a delicate hand. "He was with us but for a few moments. Your key was not mentioned, and we did not have the time to inquire about anything other than that which he revealed to us. We were simply asked to watch for you, and protect you. And so I have followed you to fulfill that oath."

"Protect me from what?" he asked.

"I do not know," Juno replied. "Please, we must be making our way soon. Let us gather your belongings and break camp. We will have much time for conversation in the hours of travel ahead of us."

And so it was that after camp was struck that Simon found himself stepping down a steep hillside painted red and orange in the morning light. The stoney hills were strewn with small rocks and large boulders that cast long shadows in the early light. Simon could not seem to take a step without kicking pebbles and creating terrible noise. Juno, on the other hand, stepped so lightly that sometimes Simon had to turn to see if she was still beside him.

The world seemed more expansive up in the foothills, with little above them and few trees save for the small groves of pines dotted across the foothills like patches on an old quilt. It was easy for Simon to feel exposed and vulnerable, though the sunlight was a welcome change to the dark, confining travels through the Aldwode and Drakewook from the earlier part of the week.

Lunch was a simple meal of berries and root vegetables that Juno had masterfully procured and prepared in her small iron pan over a bed of burning twigs and leaves. Water was scarce, but they managed to find a small stream of snowmelt that trickled down from the peaks above along an old weathered path in the rocky hillside.

Much of their travels that day were in silence, though small conversation took place whenever they stopped for food or water. But early in the afternoon, as the trail they followed began to lead them lower down the mountains and toward the flat lands of the plains, Juno began to speak freely again.

"The dwarves are dangerous beings," she said as he helped her climb over a larger boulder that blocked their path. "Your plan might not be as simple as you believe it to be."

"In what way?" he asked. "How complicated can it be to show them my key and ask them to tell me about it?"

Juno laughed softly as she hopped down from the boulder to stand beside him. "It is never a simple matter, asking questions of dwarves. And you never, under any circumstances, allow them to hold something valuable to you. The odds are never in your favor that you will ever see that object again."

"They would steal from someone?" Simon asked in shock.

"Without a doubt," she replied. "Dwarves are the living incarnation of greed and pride. Mighty craftsmen and hardy workers, to be sure, but also given to covetousness. They have a hunger deep inside them that drives them to do horrible things."

"Are they safe, then? Should I reconsider speaking to them?"

"No one is safe, Simon, not even me," she smiled as she said it. "Trust is knowing you are safe with someone, however dangerous they might be to others. We should not seek to remove the obstacles, but to build the trust. I will help you get the information you need from the dwarves, but you will have to trust me, and heed my words carefully. Do you understand?"

Simon nodded. The pair stepped carefully over a wide fissure in the rock face of the hill before continuing south. More trees loomed ahead, though they were still far off in the distance.

"Now," Juno added, "another characteristic of dwarves that is important to understand is that they are intensely possessive and protective of their belongings. They do not part with their possessions easily, and that means that we must expect trouble from them when they see your key. Even if it was crafted for someone in particular, and paid for fairly, the dwarves might very well expect it to be returned to them."

"Well, I have no intention of handing it over to them," Simon replied. "This key was given to me by my father at the moment of my birth. He thought it was important enough to pass on to me, and that makes it mine, as far as I am concerned."

"Strong-willed," Juno observed with a grin. "That is a good thing. You will need that fighting spirit when we stand before the dwarves."

"Thanks," Simon replied doubtfully. "You have not been the most encouraging. These dwarves, if I am to believe you, are greedy, ruthless thieves who aim to rob me. That makes it more difficult than you can imagine to be confident and strong."

"Ah, but you will be that and more, Simon," she replied warmly. "You will do great things. Tomorrow will be but a small part in that journey."

"If you say so," he replied sheepishly.

"I do," she quipped. "But the day is getting late. Let us make for those trees far ahead. We will set up camp for the night and begin our travels anew in the morning."

With that, the pair pressed on as their shadows grew longer and the sky darker. Simon was weary from the long hours of walking over the bare stone of the foothills, and welcomed the rest that the night would offer. He did not, however, look forward to his inevitable dealings with the dwarves at the end of this road. Simon could only hope that the answers he would find would outweigh any challenges or sacrifices he might have to make.

Chapter 13

When Simon awoke the next morning the sun had yet to pierce the eastern horizon. The sky above the tall mountain peaks was painted a deep grey with the slightest hint of orange. In the weak light of dawn it was easy to see Juno's small form seated beside the bright fire over which her small metal pan was set.

"A new day greets you, Simon," she said with a smile and a backward glance as he pulled himself up from the cold ground. "Come break fast with me."

Simon wandered slowly over to the fire, wrapping his blanket around his shoulders as he walked. The heat from the flames was refreshing, and he kept his boots off to allow his feet a chance to warm before putting them back on.

"Do you ever sleep?" he asked, poking at the fire with a long stick.

Juno laughed. It was a pleasant sound, and Simon found it as warm as the flames at his feet.

"No," she said, "I rarely need rest in the sense that you think of it. For me, what is important is quiet and stillness. The night offers both to me while the rest of the world slumbers."

Simon stretched and reached for one of the pieces of meat sizzling in the pan. He tossed it from hand to hand in an attempt to not burn his fingers, and eventually managed to take a bite after a few moments of blowing on it. The stars were still visible through the branches of the pines they had camped beneath. He did note, though, how Juno chose to build the fire out of the reach of the trees.

"What is your connection to the trees?" he asked, breaking the silence. "You called yourself a wood nymph the first time we met. What does that mean?"

"I am a shepherd and caretaker of the trees," she replied. "It is more than that, though, and difficult to explain. I give life to the trees; my sisters and I are the spirits of the groves and grottoes of this land."

"So you are a spirit?" Simon asked.

Juno paused for a moment, as if searching for the right words to give in reply. "Not a spirit in the way you would imagine, all wispy and ethereal.

The trees and I are bound together. By protecting and caring for them, I care for my sisters, and myself. That is why our task today will be so difficult."

Simon took another piece of meat from the pan. "In what way?"

"The dwarves are not people of the forest. They are lords of stone, masters of the bones of the world. My influence wanes once we leave the edges of the wilderness and enter their realm."

Simon stood and began kicking some loose soil on the dying fire. "Then perhaps it would be best if we began our day early. I would rather not have this nervous knot in my stomach any longer than necessary."

"I could not agree more," Juno said with a nod. "Let us be on our way."

The morning was late as the pair of travelers crested one of the larger foothills and caught a glimpse of the lake looming ahead of them. It was larger than Simon had thought, and shimmered in the sunlight like a pool of silver at the base of a tall, flat-faced mountain.

Though still roughly an hour away from

their destination, they could both see small, dark dots moving around the area between the lake and the mountain, like ants on a scrap of food.

"Dwarves," Juno said with little passion. "The lake is fed by hot springs from below the mountains, and the dwarves use the fresh waters for various purposes in their trades."

"Where is the fortress," Simon asked, holding one hand over his eyes to shade them from the sun. "The dragon said that they lived in the mountain."

"Yes," she answered. "The flat surface of the mountain is not natural. It has been worked and tooled by the dwarves over the vast centuries of their culture to appear the way it does today. Through the doors at the foot of the mountain one can pass into the kingdom of Fel'nagast. That is what we hope to do."

At last the foothills gave way to a low valley that ran toward the south, with high sides that rose up beside them. As the valley emptied out onto the small area of flatland that lay between them and the lake, they encountered a pair of short, heavily armored guards who stood patiently waiting for the travelers to approach.

"Halt," one of the guards grunted at them.

"You are entering uninvited into the lands of King Ogram. Declare yourselves and your purpose."

The two guards lowered their weapons, a type of long spear with a vicious-looking curved blade upon the top that Simon had never seen or heard of before, blocking the exit from the valley. They were shorter than Simon by over a head, though wider and more broad in the shoulders. Thick beards flowed over their armor and down to their belts, and some strands had been worked into braids adorned with metal beads and jewels. These were the first dwarves he had ever set his eyes upon, and there was little doubt that all he had been told about them was true.

"We seek an audience with your King," Juno announced. "We have traveled through the depths of the Aldwode and upon even the wings of a dragon to bring news and tidings to your Master. We humbly beg that you allow us to speak with him."

The two guards turned toward each other and began to speak in a language that Simon did not understand. It was full of deep, guttural sounds, and seemed harsh and cold. It was, in fact, very much like the stone of the mountain. For a moment it appeared that the dwarves were arguing with each other, but when they were finished speaking they turned back to face the travelers with calm, though also stern, faces.

"The King rarely receives visitors from outside the realm. It is very unlikely that he would wish to speak with you."

Simon began to object, but the other guard interrupted him.

"However," the second dwarven warrior said, while casting a glance toward his partner, "it is not our place to decide whom the King may deem unworthy of an audience. And so we will take you to his court, and allow you to present your case."

Simon cast a hopeful glance at Juno, but she was looking longingly over her shoulder toward the last stands of trees on the hills behind them. When she caught his eye, she offered a half-hearted smile to him.

"Now," the first dwarf barked, "you must follow us."

With that, the two guards walked away, following along a well-tended stone road that wound all the way from the mouth of the valley to the very foot of the mountain beside the lake.

The lake itself was a wonder to experience.

Heat radiated off of the waters much as it had from the skin of the great dragon, though this heat was damp and accompanied by steam and the scent of spoiled eggs. The lake was surprisingly still, and the shore was covered in small, dark stones interspersed with fragments of pottery. Then, after taking in the scope of the lake, Simon turned his eyes upon the face of the mountain, and what he saw filled him with wonder.

The face of the mountain had been carved away to create a wide, flat surface that stretched upward as far as he could see. Hundreds of ornate windows and ledges dotted the facade, some as small as one man and others as large as one of the nicer homes in Bywood. Between the scattered windows the stone had been worked to resemble pillars and arches, spanning great distances and containing recessed portions of the relief that disappeared into the shadows beyond.

There was an order to the decoration and a symmetry to the layout. Following the windows and ornamentations that covered the flat, smooth surface of the mountain, Simon slowly brought his eyes back down to his own level. There, straight ahead of them at the end of the expertly-paved road, a wide doorway had been cut with perfect angles and unnaturally straight lines into the base of the mountain.

A gate larger than anything Simon had ever witnessed before stood open, held above the vast doorway by enormous chains and a series of metal cogs and spokes. As the pair of dwarven guards led them through the threshold and into the wide entry hall, Simon looked up and shuddered to think of the force with which the gate must fall when cut lose. He stepped quickly inside.

Once through the gate Simon had expected to step into darkness, much as he had done upon entering the lair of the Red Drake. But by some ingenious use of small shafts cut deep into the mountainside, light poured into the hallway and illuminated their path far more efficiently than any torch. He glanced at Juno and noticed that she appeared visibly uncomfortable in this new environment.

The first hallway ended at a large intersection with openings for five other passageways, and without hesitation the guards led them through the central opening and deeper into the mountain. Simon could not help but wonder where each one led. After a short distance this new hallway opened up into a tall, wide chamber that was lit by four pairs of enormous braziers that blazed brightly in each corner.

At the end of yet another long hall the guards ushered Simon and Juno into a wide chamber with a set of large stone doors on the opposite wall. The doors were hung on massive iron hinges, each larger than Simon. The doors were thrice as tall as a grown man and engraved with delicate vines and intricate patterns, all centered around a depiction of dwarven warriors engaged in battle with a dragon. At the center of the scene the dragon's tail had been forged into an ornate door knocker.

One of the guards approached it swiftly and, after lifting the heavy hammer, let it drop, filling the chamber with a resounding crash that seemed like thunder. The guard then returned to stand beside the two travelers and remained still while the group waited in silence. Many long moments passed before rumbles of movement echoed from behind the door, which finally cracked open slowly with a deep creaking noise.

"Master of the Guard," intoned one of the dwarven warriors, "we bring travelers from the north who claim to have news which must be passed to our King. They claimed to have travelled here upon a dragon."

A figure stepped from the shadows beyond the doorway. He was equally short in stature as the other guards, but his greying beard was decorated with far more bejeweled objects and precious metals, denoting his lofty rank. His polished steel armor was pristine and etched with beautiful markings and designs, and at his side hung an enormous hammer that looked to have seen many battles in its day.

"Come," he boomed with a voice that sounded like fractured stone, if stone could speak, that is.

The Master of the Guard disappeared into the shadows, and Simon walked faster to keep up with the others. Through the doorway they found a wide stairway of shallow steps that wound up and out of sight to the right in a tight spiral. The steps were certainly carved for the shorter legs of the dwarves, and Simon found it difficult to pace himself on them, often skipping steps to keep up.

At the top the stairs they spilled out into a well-lit room with a high ceiling. What should have been the western wall had been cut away, leaving a large opening through which Simon could look out onto the lands beyond the dwarven kingdom. The green expanse of the Suttonwood lay far beyond the plains, and the sun could be seen hanging high in the midday sky.

    Set against the eastern wall was the most impressive sight in the chamber. An enormous throne, almost triple the size of its occupant, had been carved out of the very bones of the mountain. Polished by centuries of use and worked by the skilled hands of countless dwarven craftsmen, the throne was dark and glassy, with precious metals filling the fine lines and engravings that covered its surface.

    The figure seated upon the great black throne was heavily armored in thick plates of polished steel edged with gold. His beard was black, though almost all of it was braided and adorned in the accouterments that declared his position over the others. The armored figure was perched at the edge of the throne's stone seat, his elbows resting on his steel-clad knees, watching the pair of travelers enter the room with piercing blue eyes.

    The guards walked Simon and Juno into the center of the chamber and then silently retreated. Simon glanced at his friend for a glimpse of hope, but he found her face to be painted in worry and fear. He had expected to manage this conversation on his own, but any help from her would have been welcome. Regardless, he took a step forward and began to reach for his necklace. But before his hand could even slip under the collar of his shirt, the King jumped up from his throne.

The short, heavy figure landed only a pace or so in front of Simon, sending a loud crash echoing off of the walls as his boots slapped against the stone floor. Without a moment of hesitation or pause the dwarf reached for his sword. In one smooth motion the King drew a short, thick blade and swung it around to point at the nape of Simon's neck.

"Choose your words carefully, man-child," the King growled as he slowly moved closer, keeping the sword leveled on Simon's head all the while. "Who are you? And what business of yours could possibly have brought you here to bother the King of the Dwarves?"

Chapter 14

The Hunter's journey from the abbey had been long and laborious. He did not make camp that night, and instead traveled through the darkness to make up time he had lost while speaking to the Abbott. The following sunrise allowed him to guide Anthus toward the river Hesperus where the foliage was less dense and the terrain more passable.

He travelled along the river's edge for most of that day, with the darkness of the Aldwode to his left and the powerful swiftness of the Hesperus to his right. It felt good to walk free from the obstruction of the dense underbrush, and Anthus seemed to also welcome the reprieve. But the uninterrupted walk also allowed the Hunter to think on the words of the monk the night before.

He was told that the witch lived to the east, but beyond that general description he was left guessing for himself. The Aldwode was long and expansive from east to west, but rather narrow from north to south. His assumption was that somewhere between the northern and southern borders he would find a dwelling, but his only guide was a very old, very worn trail that ran along the river bank. The Hunter placed his hope in that assumption.

Day became night and the Hunter ventured into the edges of the forest deep enough to find a large oak with space beneath it for the two of them. He set up a meager camp without fire, and allowed himself to sleep for three or four hours before rising again at the first sign of light in the early morning sky. Then, guiding Anthus back to the rushing river, they continued on.

After hours of walking along the river the trail bent toward the trees again, taking them once again into the dense forest. Even Anthus was beginning to show the frayed edges of his patience, and the deeper they traveled into the Aldwode, the closer the branches seemed to grow, as if the forest were trying to embrace them. This, however, was an embrace the Hunter was eager to escape, though his mission took priority, and so he pushed them onward.

As the sounds of the swollen spring waters subsided behind them, another sound began to grow. At first the noise was indistinguishable from the sounds of forest life; the creaking of old limbs, the scratching of bark and the occasional animal hidden in the underbrush. But after a few moments it became clear that the sound was something unusual for the forest.

It was the sound of a dog barking. Multiple dogs, if the Hunter's ears were not deceiving him. And so he slipped from Anthus' back and led the horse off the path and into the deep of the wooded maze that was the Aldwode, all the while keeping his focus bent toward the dogs.

After a few more paces it became clear that he was heading in the right direction. He pushed through half a dozen wild hedges that seemed to have grown with the express purpose of keeping him from traveling farther, and once through them he stepped into a clearing. At the center of the clearing he found the two dogs, chained to a large oak tree that grew in front of a small, weary-looking house.

Anthus did not flinch at the sight of the dogs, but did however twitch his tail at the hovel they seemed to be guarding. The Hunter patted his faithful horse on the shoulder and hung the reins over a low branch. Then, moving carefully and with full awareness of his surroundings, he proceeded toward the shack.

As the Hunter approached the front of the house, carefully staying clear of the two patrolling dogs, a figure emerged from the doorway. It was that of an old woman, bent and weathered with age, with a crooked nose and bushy eyebrows. Her skirt of brown wool blended well with the forest, and her shoulders were wrapped in a thin white shawl.

"Quit 'yer noise-makin'!" she shouted at the dogs as she descended the two steps down from the porch to the brown soil of the ground.

"If I have t'come out here ev'ry..." she began, but stopped upon seeing him.

The Hunter was accustomed to receiving second glances from strangers, most commonly due to his unusual attire. The silver, bearded mask and antlered helm almost always took people by surprise, helping him to stand out in a crowd. Which is why he generally avoided crowds when at all possible.

But this old woman cast a different sort of glance at him. Her's was one of understanding, and her eyes seemed to sparkle when they settled on him. It took only an instant, but the Hunter was certain he had found the witch that he had been seeking.

"I was expectin' you," she quipped. "Though I'm not quite sure what one so important as the King's Hunter himself would want from old Hekate."

The Hunter stepped closer, but was careful to keep a safe distance from both the dogs and the witch. The Aldwode was full of magical creatures if a person knew where to look, but none were as dangerous as a witch, and this one was older than most he knew of.

"I seek information, woman," he said hoarsely through his mask. "But I warn you to keep your tricks to yourself, and if you cooperate I will spare your life."

The old woman smiled, though her face seemed tired. "You are too kind, Hunter. Your mercy is most unexpected, and I'll do m'best to aid your quest. What can I answer fer ya."

"I have heard tell that you are far older than you appear," he said. "Tell me about your dealings with King Toren long ago."

"I am old, that is true," she replied. "But my memory isn't what it used t'be, I'm afraid."

The Hunter knew it was unwise to spend

more than a short amount of time with the witch, and that the more she spoke, the more deceit she would be able to spin. He quickly drew one of the long, vicious-looking knives that he kept hidden away within his black cloak, and leveled the tip of the blade with the witch's throat.

"I will ask once more only," he demanded, "Tell me of the task which Toren set you to complete. What was your roll in the hiding away of the crown."

"I ne'er touched the crown!" she responded, shying away from the blade. "I was merely a messenger and a go-between fer the King."

"And what task did the King set before you, then?"

The old woman shook her head. "Nothing of consequence, I'm sure. I was asked to send messages to a few of the most renowned craftsmen in the land. But the messages were sealed and ne'er passed before my eyes, I swear it!"

The Hunter lowered the blade, pleased with his progress so far. "I have been informed that you were asked to gather materials for the creation of the crown's hiding place. What tasks did you complete for King Toren beside the delivery of the messages?"

The witch kicked at the dirt with one of her feet before looking back at the Hunter. "Gold. I delivered some gold fer the King. In exchange fer a package. But I don't know what the package contained. I was young, y' understand? I hadn't come into my own yet. And the King had promised me such great power if only I would take care of some matters fer him."

He nodded, understanding her. "Where did Toren send you?" he asked.

"The Drakewood," she replied. "He sent me t' find the dragon, the Red Drake, to purchase something of importance, something one of my messages had evidently requested to be made ready."

She laughed as she recalled the task, and looked off into the trees when she began again. "I had ne'er seen so much gold before in m'life, and ne'er have since. It took four horses, four of the King's best steads, mind you, to pull the carriage that held the chest of gold, that's how big it were."

"So you were asked by King Toren to take a chest of gold to the great dragon of the Drakewood? For what purpose?"

The witch shook her head again.

"Honestly, Hunter, I was kept as uninformed as the King could manage. 'Take this gold,' he said to me, 'and deliver it to the Drake himself. Bring back that which he gives to you in return for this great treasure.'"

"And did you do as he asked?" he said, glancing around the clearing for a sign that the witch had kept the gold and used it for her own gain. But she nodded immediately.

"I took that treasure farther than I had ever travelled before, across dense woodland and wide river. And when I reached the lair of the great beast himself, I found him waiting for me, seated outside the entrance to his mountain abode.

"He sniffed at my horses like a starving man inspecting a loaf of fresh bread, I'll tell y' that, Hunter. But he was courteous enough, and took the gold in exchange for a package, which he produced from a fold in his hide."

"What did the package contain?" the Hunter asked hopefully, counting on the witch's propensity for dishonesty to have led her to peak inside to discover what it was.

"I never found out," she replied. The disbelieving look from the Hunter caused the witch to sigh. "I tried, of course. Are you pleased to know that? I could not understand how something could be worth exchanging for so much gold. But the package was enchanted beyond my skills, and though I tried the entire journey back t' the King, I was unable t' open it."

The Hunter felt defeated. He had travelled so far to discover the hidden location of the crown, only to be met with mystery and incomplete information. He had begun to wonder if this quest would be his last. But before he could allow himself to drift deeper into doubt and pity, the witch spoke again.

"Seek the dragon, Hunter," she said. "The Red Drake guards his lair to this day. Perhaps he'd be able t' tell ya what it was that King Toren had requested from him so long ago. I honestly doubt he'll be able to tell you where that crown was hid, but it's safe to assume that whatever was in that package could point you there."

"I do not trust you, witch, and never will," the Hunter replied. "But I find a grain of sense in those words. You have offered me hope where I thought none existed. For that, I will allow you to live."

The witch bowed to the Hunter and then smiled. "How kind of you, great Hunter," she said dramatically. "If only everyone could be as merciful as you." A hint of some hidden truth glimmered in her eyes.

"Hold your tongue," the Hunter hissed through his mask. He brought the knife blade back up toward her throat and took one step closer. "I expect to find answers in the days to come. But if you have falsely steered me toward danger and failure, I will return for you. I will not suffer a witch to make a fool of me."

As he turned to go, the witch waved her hand one last time, catching his attention. "Tell yer fortune before y' go?" she asked, pointing back toward the porch of her weary house. The Hunter followed her crooked finger to an oddly shaped basket resting on the porch. It was oval in shape, with a small opening on the top that was stuffed with a wet rag of some sort. "The spirits never lie."

"No," he replied. "My fate is in my hands, and mine alone."

"Of course," she replied with a knowing smile. "Of course it is. Fair ye' well, then, Hunter."

He walked back to Anthus as quickly as he could, and did not turn back as he led the horse again into the thickness of the ancient forest. Then, setting his course toward the east, he set off to find the answers he sought.

Chapter 15

"Stop," Juno said as she stepped between Simon and the blade, bringing her hands up in one slow movement. "You must forgive our intrusion, for we have need of your great wisdom and knowledge."

"Must?" the dwarven king growled. "I must? Little girl, I must do nothing you ask of me. It is you who must. You must explain yourselves, and be quick, for my time is better spent watching the sunset than listening to intruders in my realm."

The king lowered his mighty sword and replaced it in the sheath hanging at his side, and then turned back toward his throne. He moved with slow, steady steps and took his seat between his attendants and guards, heavily armored soldiers holding long halberds and shields. Once he was settled, the king motioned again at the travelers.

"Speak!"

Juno looked again at Simon, and the pair exchanged knowing glances. Finally it was Juno who turned and responded to the king.

"Your Majesty," she began, "we have traveled from the wilds of the Aldwode to find answers to riddles we are unable to solve. My friend Simon and I seek knowledge of something crafted by your people. Something forged long ago that you perhaps sold or gifted to a mighty king of Men."

"Ha!" the king cried. "Our people would never give something valuable away. There is always a cost. What do you seek to know?"

"This young man," she said, pointing toward Simon, "was born to parents who did not live to raise him themselves. They died the night of his birth, but not before passing something on to him that he has carried with himself every moment of his life ever since. That object has led him on a quest to discover who he might truly be."

Simon stepped forward at this point, and placed a hand on Juno's shoulder. She turned toward him for a moment, catching a reassuring look in his eyes, and then stepped back. Simon then approached the throne.

"I left my home, Your Majesty, in hopes that I could discover where this heirloom came from, and in that way learn more about who I am meant to become. I travelled deep through the ancient Aldwode and far into the dark lair of the great worm himself, the Red Drake. I left the dragon's lair his friend, and rode upon his back through the sky to reach your lands. For I believe that it is you who hold the answer to my mystery."

The king rested his bearded head on the tips of his fingers and leaned forward on the throne. He peered at Simon for an unbearable length of time before speaking again.

"Most impressive, young man-child," he said. "There are few in my long memory that have called the dragon a friend, and none have had the opportunity to ride upon its very wings. If I were honest with you, though, I would make it clear that the Red Drake is no friend of the dwarves. Because of him our numbers have dwindled, and our people risk vanishing from this world. But to have subdued the beast yourself is quite the achievement. Your quest must indeed be important."

"It is, Your Majesty," Simon replied with a nod. "The dragon taught me something I had not known about my heirloom, and that is why I am here before you. According to him, the object I carry is of dwarven make."

"Dwarven?" the king cried out. "Then it was surely stolen from our lands, taken from us in the night or robbed from our very storerooms. You are certainly exceedingly wise and prudent for your years to seek to return the item to our care."

"I believe Your Majesty misunderstands my friend," Juno interrupted, stepping forward again to stand beside Simon. "He has come here to learn more about the object, not to return it."

The king choked on his words and writhed in frustration. He did not appear to be the sort of person who reacted well to the denial of his requests, and was soon back on his feet moving toward them.

"Show them," Juno whispered harshly at Simon as the king came closer. "Quickly!"

Simon fumbled with the chain around his neck as he tried to pull the key from inside his shirt. Taking the small object between his thumb and forefinger, he held it up for the king to see. All at once murmurs broke out around them, and the king stopped.

"I wish to know the story of this key," Simon requested. "This is the key my father gave to me when I was born. I believe it is the key to discovering who I am."

The king turned and waved one of his guards over. A younger-looking dwarf quickly ran to his side, and the king whispered something into his ear. At once the guard was gone, nearly tumbling down the staircase into the fortress below. Then the king returned his attention to Simon, stepping close enough to touch the key.

"This is most unusual. It resembles the work of dwarves, but I have never seen its like. It is far older than any of us here," he began. "Does it have any markings?"

Simon nodded and turned the key around, exposing the engraving for the king to inspect as well.

"Ah," the king exclaimed, "it is engraved. This text seems very similar to an ancient form of dwarvish lettering that we refer to as Old Hand. The masters of old were accomplished in that type of rounded longhand script, something our people seem to have lost the patience for attempting. It has been a very long time since one of our people engraved in the Old Hand, though I cannot be certain what that means for your key."

The king looked at Simon and then back at the key. His eyes had a darkness to them, almost like an emptiness or a hunger, and Simon could not help but to lean back slightly while pressing the key harder between his thumb and fingertips. Just then the sound of footsteps from the staircase drew all of their eyes.

The younger guard had returned, completely out of breath and panting as he mounted the final steps. Following closely behind him was a new face, though not one belonging to a guard. This dwarf was stooped low with age, making him look even smaller than the other dwarves in the chamber, as short of stature as they themselves were.

His beard was cut short and was absent of any decoration that those of the warrior profession seemed to flaunt. Instead, this figure was wrapped in an elaborate robe of emerald and silver, and he wore a small, round cap on the top of his head. As he climbed the last of the stairs Simon could see a large book tucked under the figure's arm.

"Gollath," the king said, "thank you for coming so quickly."

The older dwarf nodded and approached them slowly. "It is always an honor to serve you, my Lord. And it is not very often that I have the opportunity to identify something lost or forgotten. Now, where is the object?"

The king cast a glance at Simon, who had lowered his arm instinctively and wrapped his hand around the key. Simon startled, as if waking from a dream, and then held the heirloom up for the scholar to inspect.

"Interesting," the old dwarf muttered as he leaned toward the key. "I have never seen anything like it in all my years. It is similar to our own craft, but different somehow. I am unsure of its origin."

"Consult your records, then," the king offered, motioning to the large tome the scholar had carried up with him.

"Of course," he replied as if remembering something he had forgotten. "The Book of Making may have some notation regarding the piece, if it was forged here."

"Where else could it have been forged?" Simon asked.

"Any one of a handful of ancient dwarven cities. Two were deep within the Ironbrood Mountains to the north, and another was built under the mountain now inhabited by the Red Drake. They have slowly slipped from our hands, with all but Fel'nagast lost to us now, and with them their Books of Making."

Juno approached again. "What do the

books record?"

"Craftsmen would describe the piece they had completed," the king replied as he watched the scholar turn the pages of the book. "Often times with accompanying drawings or even instructions to replicate the object. Most, however, would simply scribble the name or description of the item along with a date."

"Here," the scholar interrupted. "I believe I may have found something."

Simon leaned over to see if he could read the page, but it was covered with symbols and characters that were foreign to him. Juno did the same but only shook her head at the unusual runes. There were, however, a handful of drawings on the aged parchment, though the ink had faded to a faint grey, making them difficult to see clearly. The scholar had pointed to a collection of lines that was clearly meant to represent a key.

Simon's key.

"Well?" the king exclaimed. "What does it say, old fool!"

"This page records a drawing of the key which you can clearly see here," he said, pointing at the sketch. "But there are no records on the page that the key was the object crafted."

"Then why is it drawn on the page?" the king asked impatiently.

The scholar did not look up, but continued to run his finger over the odd characters on the page while moving his lips. "The key was brought here by someone else, though it does not say who, and a lock was fashioned to receive the key. A lock that was mounted within a stone box."

Simon turned to Juno with a confused expression. "My key was used to craft a box? What does that even mean?"

The nymph shook her head. "I do not know. But perhaps the Book can tell us more? Something that can help guide our search for an answer?"

The scholar shook his head. "It is difficult to translate. The character for 'box' could mean many things, such as 'chest' or 'storeroom'."

"Well that's not helpful at all," Simon muttered, putting the key back inside his shirt and turning to look at the afternoon sun outside the wide window.

"Wait!" the scholar exclaimed. "Whatever the container truly was seems to have been portable enough to have been delivered to a specific place."

"Where?" asked Juno and Simon at the same moment.

"Northwest," he replied. "To a grove near the fork in the southern arm of the Estin River. But that is all it tells me."

Juno smiled. "Groves are my specialty, Simon. I think I know where we need to go. But we have a long road to get there, and should make our way as soon as possible."

Simon nodded, but the king nudged the scholar aside and placed his hand on the hilt of his sword.

"I do not think I will be allowing that key to leave my kingdom," he growled with a hungry gleam in his eyes. "What was once my people's will be returned to me at once."

Simon stared at the sword in disbelief. He had evidently underestimated the level of greed that consumed the king's heart. He stepped backward but stumbled into the immoveable form of a royal guard. Others appeared around them, each lowering his halberd to point at the two travelers.

Juno cast a distressed expression toward the scholar, but he shied away, pretending to be too busy running his fingers over the text of the page again.

"Wait!" she cried out. "You cannot do this. This is not right!"

"What is right," snapped the king in reply, "is for that which belongs to my culture to be returned at once. Hand over the key."

Juno stepped in front of Simon, who put his hand over his chest as if to protect the key from the king. His mind was racing with fear and panic at the thought of losing the only remaining piece of who he truly was. Without the key, his past would be left a mystery.

Just then, an idea began to form in Simon's mind. "Wait," he said. He glanced around at the circle of guards and the sharp weapons that were pointed at them. "I have a proposition."

The king considered for a moment before responding. "I am listening," he finally said.

"I understand that you feel that the key belongs to you because somewhere deep in your past it was created by your ancestors. But my father passed it on to me when I was born, and judging by its age that was not the first time the key was inherited. To me, this key is a birthright."

"I fail to see your point, man-child," the king responded. "We have no way of proving whether this key was stolen from its maker, or sold."

No," Simon replied, "we do not. So I propose a trade. You allow me to keep the key, so that I may follow the trail it has left in hopes that it may lead me to my destiny. And in return I will tell the Red Drake to stop hunting your people."

"Ha!" the king laughed. "No man can control a dragon."

"I can," Simon replied. "The Red Drake owes me a debt of gratitude, and I will ask him to honor that debt. He will have no choice but to obey what I ask of him."

The king thought on the offer for a moment. Simon could clearly see the struggle on the face of the dwarf, and understood why. Being greedy and possessive by nature, the king obviously wanted the key back. But the safety of his people and culture was also imperative. Simon could only hope that his offer was attractive enough to him.

"You are a stranger to me, and your word does not have weight in these halls," the king began. "But you offer something that I could never give to my people on my own. And because of that, I will accept."

Simon heard Juno gasp beside him, and he

smiled in relief. "Thank you, your Majesty. I promise that I will keep my word and speak to the dragon once I find this mysterious stone container. He will hunt your people no longer."

The king nodded and then waved all but one of the guards away. "Please escort these travelers out of the city," he said to him sternly. "They are free to leave as they wish, though the faster they travel, the less likely I will be to change my mind."

Simon looked at Juno, harried by the events but relieved to have their freedom returned.

"Thank you again, your Majesty," Simon replied.

The decent down the stairs and journey back through the great hallways of the city seemed to take forever with the constant worry that the king might change his mind hanging over them like a cloud. But they soon emerged from the mountain to see the late afternoon sun reflected in the still waters of the lake, and the road extending out before them.

Simon turned to thank the guard for guiding them back down through the fortress, but he had already left them. Still afraid that the king would change his mind, they quickly made their way west, following the paved road as far is it took them until they finally had to step off into the tall grasses of the plains as it curved off to the south. Setting their coarse for the dark line of forest on the horizon, the pair began the next leg of their journey.

  Simon turned and glanced back toward the sheer face of the ancient mountain home of the dwarves one last time, and then offered a hopeful smile to Juno. They might not yet have the answer they were hoping to discover, but it was clear that their path was leading them ever closer to the truth. It was this hope that gave Simon the strength to turn back around and begin walking toward the setting sun.

  They had only taken a few steps, however, when a voice called out to them from the distance. Turning to the north they saw the shape of a horse and rider approaching, becoming more clear as it drew near. Suddenly Simon realized who it was that had hailed them.

  "Sir Lovelace?" he exclaimed questioningly at the approaching knight. "Is that really you?"

Chapter 16

The Hunter pushed himself, and Anthus, hard through the night. The information he learned from the witch Hekate had given him hope that he still might complete his quest and return to his master King Telarius with his honor intact. Stepping across the Estin earlier in the morning, he had left the dense Aldwode behind in favor of the more sparsely wooded Drakewood, and as he did so his spirit was lifted.

The path east from the river rose steadily toward the mountain that loomed in the distance, occasionally visible through breaks in the branches above. A thin stream of smoke drifted out of some invisible opening near the peak, letting the Hunter know that the dragon was indeed home. Instead of falling into fear and doubt about whether he could even discover the information he needed from the dangerous beast, he set his mind on the task at hand and guided Anthus swiftly and expertly through the quiet woodlands.

The Hunter moved much like he always did, silently and smoothly working his way between large trees and boulders warped by intense heat. He noted that the landscape looked as if it had been scorched to the soil generations ago and then left to claw its way back to survival. Knowing what he did about dragons, he was certain that this was the work of the Red Drake.

After passing through a series of clearings, the Hunter noticed that the mountain was clearly visible a short distance ahead, and chose to leave Anthus near a small stream while he continued on foot. The foothills rose more steeply now and soon he was able to look back to see the last of the trees falling away. Soon after, the ground leveled off and he was standing at the foot of the mountain.

The entrance to the dragon's lair was nothing more or less than the Hunter expected, having seen other dragons in his lifetime. The Red Drake had chosen a dormant volcano with a wide opening at the base, and through years of use and subtle working had shaped for himself a grand entryway. Confident and determined, the Hunter approached quickly and stepped inside.

He made no effort to silence the scuffing of his boots on the rough floor of the passageway, and his eyes quickly adjusted to the darkness as the daylight behind him faded away. After a few moments of walking he began to see the glow of the lair ahead. Inside, curled up in the center of the enormous chamber, the dragon lay sleeping, motionless yet imposing.

It was only as the Hunter stepped through the threshold into the lair itself that the dragon's eyes opened and settled on him.

"Who are you?" the creature asked calmly.

"I am the King's Hunter," he replied. "Know that killing me will not endear you to the Iron King's heart."

"You are children, playing at make-believe," the dragon said. "You pretend that centuries have not passed before my eyes. I know of only one Iron King, and he no longer walks these woods. What you and your master make play at is merely a fantasy. You are shadows of those who came before you."

The Hunter did not expect the beast to be so well spoken or opinionated, but he did not intend to allow the beast to lull him with his words.

"I believe you do not give us enough credit," he offered in reply. "The King is a man of great power and influence."

"That does not, however, explain why he would need you to travel to my mountain and rob me. How powerful can a man be when he must steal to build his own kingdom. Leave, thief, before I make a meal of you."

The dragon slowly stood, pulling all four muscular legs underneath itself before standing to tower over the Hunter. The Red Drake lowered its head to look more closely at the man, and then snorted loudly.

"I am not here to steal from you," he replied while glancing around the chamber, "though I am certain that many of the items that make up your hoard once belonged to various rulers of Varelia, so it is debatable who the true thief might be. No, I have come seeking answers and information."

The dragon turned away and sat back on his hind legs as if he had lost his interest in the conversation. "I am not a wizard or advisor, Hunter of the King. I am a dragon."

"Yes," the Hunter replied. "You are a dragon, and thus you are long lived and have born witness to many events that even history itself has forgotten."

The dragon nodded. "This is true."

"I have come to inquire about one of those events, a moment that time and legend have nearly forgotten. Specifically, I wish to ask you about a visit once paid to you long ago by a witch, during the reign of King Toren. That very same witch has told me as much, but a witch's word can rarely be trusted, so I have come to find the source of her tale."

The dragon thought for a moment, the effort visible to the Hunter's experienced eyes. After a moment the beast spoke again, though he looked off into the darkness of the chamber's invisible edges.

"I recall the witch, yes," he said. "She travelled in a coach pulled by some of the finest horses I have ever seen. They would have made a delicious meal had I not been obligated to send her back swiftly and safely."

The Hunter was relieved that the details matched those given to him by the witch Hekate. "And what did your encounter with her entail, if I can ask?"

"She came to make a transaction," the dragon recalled. "The horses pulled a coach that contained gold. An entire chest of gold. It was payment for a service I rendered to the Iron King upon his request."

The Hunter began to feel even more hopeful. The witch appeared to have been telling the truth about her journey to the dragons lair and the gold she delivered. Something important had taken place, and he was certain that the details of the event would eventually lead him to the lost crown.

"What was this transaction about?" he asked impatiently. "And why are you so slow to offer up the answers I seek?"

"Patience, Hunter of the King," the dragon replied. "I am recalling and recounting something that I have never shared with anyone else in the centuries that have passed since that day. To tell the story properly is to remember the details accurately."

"Fair enough," he responded. "Please carry on, then."

The dragon nodded and continued. "I remember that I had received a message months earlier, a message carried to me by a raven, that requested I locate something in my treasure hoard, something that King Toren wanted from me.

"Of course, nothing is free, even when a King is requesting it, and so I had replied and told him that whatever he sought would require a payment larger than he could possibly agree to send. I remember months passing by without hearing from the King or his messenger, assuming that my offer had frightened them away to find what they needed elsewhere. And then, one day, the witch mysteriously arrived and offered more gold to me than I could hope to gather in a century of diligent hunting."

"What did the King want from you?" the Hunter asked.

"A key," the dragon replied.

The Hunter paused, caught off guard by the answer. "A key?" he asked. "The Iron King sent a witch to deliver a fortune in gold in exchange for a key?"

The dragon nodded once.

"What can you tell me of this key?" the Hunter asked. "Where did it come from?"

"I do not know where the key originally came from," the dragon answered. "I only remember finding it amongst a great hoard that I fairly won from an old and dying dragon far to the north. I was young and brash in those days, and challenged a revered male many times my own age.

"Rag'oren he was called, the Great One, and was the forefather of all the northern drakes. But he fell easily to me, and I brought his hoard south to my own lair. It was shortly after that when I stumbled upon the key, but I cannot tell you how King Toren would have known that I possessed it."

"But it was clear from the price he paid that he wanted badly to have it," the Hunter offered.

"Yes," he replied. "Whether because of want or desire, Toren was deeply motivated."

"Did the witch ever tell you what purpose the key was meant to serve for Toren?" he asked.

"No," the dragon replied. "The message I received only contained a drawing of the key and a short note offering to purchase it from me. The raven who carried the note was not of the speaking variety, you see. Though looking back, I am certain that I could have asked for even more gold if I had known what the true purpose of the key was. The cost of an item is often intrinsically related to the level of need within the buyer.

"The witch, though, was more forthcoming with information. She was young and eager to learn, and made mention of the determination that Toren possessed regarding some secret task.

The key, she informed me, played a central part in this task. The quintessential key, one might say."

"Indeed," the Hunter agreed. "But she said no more than that?"

"Only that I was but one of a small handful of recipients of the King's messages." The dragon paused thoughtfully for a moment. "No," he said, shaking his enormous head, "there is nothing else that I can recall. I apologize."

"No need," he replied. "You have been most helpful. At the very least you have helped confirm that the witch's words to me were true. I only wish I could have learned the reason for Toren's interest in a small key from a dragon's hoard. Following a trend that is becoming quite common for me as of late, I shall be leaving here with more questions than answers."

"I would sorely like to have it back," the dragon muttered as if to himself. "Something about that key set it apart from all the other keys scattered about my lair in a way that I cannot begin to describe. No other key has managed to accomplish that. Although..." he trailed off.

The Hunter had been about to turn and leave the dragon to wrestle alone with his musings and regret, but something in the creature's voice caught his ear. "Although...?"

"Well," the dragon began, "perhaps it was nothing. But I recently saw another key, one that was remarkably similar, now that I think back upon them both. Remarkably similar. Very ancient in appearance, and oddly forged."

"In what way was it similar?" the Hunter pressed. "Or better yet, how was this key different from the first?"

"That is perhaps the easiest question you have asked me yet," the dragon replied. "The difference would be clearly visible to anyone, for carved into the surface of one side was one small word: destiny."

The Hunter froze. "Did you say 'destiny'?"

"I did," replied the dragon. "It was expertly inscribed, and ancient, but very easy to read."

"And who possessed this key that you saw?" The Hunter could not stop his heart from racing now, and his mind was beginning to swim with countless thoughts and questions. "Tell me about this person."

"A young man and a knight," the dragon replied. "Though I frightened the knight away. The young man selflessly helped me with an old injury. Had it not been for his generosity, I most certainly would have eaten him and taken the key for myself."

"I am sorry," the Hunter interrupted. "I believe I now have the answer I was looking for." With that, he turned and began to leave. The dragon watched as the man walked swiftly toward the threshold of the passageway that led from the main chamber to the mountain's entrance beyond.

"Thank you, Master Drake," the Hunter called out as he quickly stepped into the tunnel. "You have helped me more than you will ever understand."

The dragon sat in stunned silence as the sound of the man's footsteps slowly faded into the darkness beyond. Then, certain that he had departed, the creature lowered himself to the floor, curled his tail about himself and closed his eyes to sleep once more.

Chapter 17

Simon pushed another small branch into the fire and nudged the embers near the bottom to help the orange glow intensify. It had been a little over one full day since their departure from Fel'nagast, and the hard day of traveling had worn his body down. Though the plains west of the mountains were flat and open, the ground was hard and his feet ached to the bone.

The day had its fair share of events, though. Their first evening together was slightly awkward as Sir Lovelace struggled to believe that Juno was both real and harmless to them. The knight seemed to display a certain distrust or dislike toward the wood nymph, and Simon often found himself managing the tension between them through that first day together.

Night had started to fall a little over an hour before, and as the stars began to pierce the deep grey sky one by one, the travelers had made their way to the eastern edge of the Suttonwood and begun to prepare a small camp to spend the night. This being their second night as a group, everyone knew what their roles were, and fell easily into them. Juno went off in search of something they could all eat, Sir Lovelace guided Billy over to one of the larger trees and made sure the area was safe for them, and Simon ventured out into the forest a few paces in search of usable firewood.

Finding quality kindling had been difficult during their passage through the plains. There were trees, of course, but they were scattered so far apart and lacked the dense, thick character one could find within the borders of the Aldwode. Simon learned the night before that it was necessary to supplement what little wood he could find with bundles of dried grass, something far more common on the plains than trees.

Here, though, firewood was plentiful, and it took only a few moments before Simon found his way back to camp, his arms heavy-laden with fallen branches and dried bark. He found Juno setting spark to a small pile of twigs and leaves, and she looked relieved as he approached with something more useful to burn.

When Sir Lovelace returned from setting up Billy for the night, he joined Simon and Juno around the fire. Dinner was a small handful of prairie fowl that Juno somehow had managed to catch. The mysterious nymph continued to surprise Simon with her ability to obtain what they needed from the world around them.

While Juno watched the birds sizzle over the flames, Simon glanced at the old knight across the fire and decided now was the time to have the conversation he had waited all day to have. Sir Lovelace fidgeted where he sat and looked entirely unable to make himself comfortable, and it occurred to Simon that perhaps the knight had looked forward to this moment as little as he had.

"So," he began uncomfortably, "where did you go when you ran away from the dragon? You never came back for me."

The knight looked uncomfortable, shifting his gaze back and forth around Simon but never settling on him. He stammered for a moment before answering. He could not help but feel like Sir Lovelace was ashamed.

"That beast was going to kill me," he offered defensively. "You did not see the look in its eye, lad. Wild, that monster was. I fled for my life. I am glad to see that you made it out alive as well."

"The dragon did not seem overly vicious to

me," Simon replied. "And I did not run as you did. I stayed."

Sir Lovelace looked horrified. "You what?"

"I stayed," he repeated. "The dragon was injured, and I offered to help him take care of the wound. I pulled this out of the bottom of his foot."

Simon reached around to where his pack lay beside his blanket and pulled the sword free from the straps. He unwrapped the cloth he had covered the weapon with and handed it to the knight. Sir Lovelace gasped in awe as the polished steel blade shimmered in the light of the fire.

"My sword!" he cried out.

"Your...? You mean you were the one who left this in the dragon's foot?"

"The one and the same," the knight replied, proudly puffing up his chest. "And had it not gotten stuck I would have finished the creature off that day. Ah, how I have missed this blade."

"Keep it," Simon offered. He had tired of the added weight in his pack, and never felt completely comfortable with the sharp blade so near to his body. "It was yours before, so it is yours again."

The old knight beamed at him and slapped him on the back. "Thank you, Simon. What an unexpected surprise!" His voice trailed off as thoughts seemed to wash over his face.

"I hate to interrupt," said Juno, "but we should discuss our plans for tomorrow before it gets too late."

Sir Lovelace glared back at the nymph, but she failed to notice. She had taken one of the sticks from the pile of kindling and then brushed a patch of dirt smooth with her hand. With the stick she drew a winding line that branched into two separate lines.

"The River Estin runs south through the Suttonwood before the Brance splits off westward. Right at this fork in the river," she emphasized her words by pointing the stick to the place where the Estin divided, "there is an ancient grove, protected and revered by my people, known as the Alsean Grove. That is our destination."

"And this mysterious stone box will be waiting for us there?" Sir Lovelace asked with a doubtful tone.

"I do not know," she replied. "It has been a very long time since I have set foot in the Alsea, and I do not remember much more than the sound of the river and the beauty of the open clearing."

"Well then," Simon said as he moved away

from the fire to climb onto his blanket, "I do not know about the two of you, but my body aches from walking so far, and I will need all the rest I can manage if I am to make it another day. Perhaps we should all turn in for the night."

"Agreed," added the knight, who stood and walked off in search of his bedding.

"Good night, Juno," Simon offered. "I hope your night is restful as well."

The wood nymph smiled warmly as she settled in beside the fire. "Thank you, Simon. I hope the same for you."

The travelers made quick work of the remaining portion of their journey as the sun rose that morning. The Suttonwood was much less dense than the Aldwode, though it was clear that it was equally ancient, if not older. Juno guided them to a clear trail that ran west and north, and the cool morning hours passed swiftly.

Soon the sounds of running water cut through the quiet of the forest, and the travelers stepped out of the trees onto the bank of a waterway not much wider than a small river, but more shallow. Sir Lovelace allowed Billy to cross first, trusting the horse's instincts to find the safest path across the riverbed, and soon they had all navigated their way across.

Moments after having crossed the river the three travelers passed through a thin cluster of trees to step into a wide opening in the forest. The ground was covered with small dark green leaves and dotted with white flowers, while the sky was wide and blue above. Across the clearing Simon could see the Estin flowing toward them before the Brance River forked to the left, cutting the grove off from the rest of the wooded land on either side of them.

"The Alsean Grove," said Juno with more than a little joy in her voice. "Welcome to one of the places held most sacred by my sisters."

"It is quiet and empty," Sir Lovelace added, "but I fail to see what makes this place so special."

Juno frowned toward the knight and then walked away from them into the center of the grove. Simon followed, glancing around the open space for any sign of the container they had travelled so far to find. It took a moment of searching, but soon he sighted a small stone protruding from the dark leaves of the flowers, far off on the outer edge of the clearing.

"Here!" he cried out as he ran toward the stone. "I found something!"

The others joined him quickly, and as they approached Simon dropped to his knees and began to push the leaves and moss aside to uncover the base of the stone. It was small, no larger around than a fence post, and only as tall as Simon's shin. But it was clearly unnatural to the location, obviously shaped and worked by hand.

"Could this be it?" Sir Lovelace asked. "It is not much to look at, that much is true."

Simon agreed, and could not shake the feeling that he had missed something. He glanced to his left and right, inspecting more of the grove, and suddenly pointed a few paces away.

"Another one," he said, and then continued moving his finger until he found another equally distanced away. "And another."

"Quick," Juno interrupted. "Search the entire outer edge; I have a feeling there are more of these stones."

Simon watched as Sir Lovelace and Juno walked in opposite directions, shouting out as they each encountered more of the small stone posts protruding from the earth beneath the carpet of flowers. After a moment of pacing and counting,

Juno ran back over to him.

"There are ten, Simon," she said as she stopped beside him. "They form a ring around the grove. I do not know why I have never seen them before, but the flowers here bloom all throughout the year, hiding them from the casual observer."

"What do you think they are for?" Simon asked. "They can't all be the container that the Book of Making spoke of, can they? And they seem too small to hold anything."

"I agree," she replied. "Whatever the container is, it must be hidden elsewhere. Perhaps it is buried somewhere in this clearing?"

Simon nodded. "We will need Sir Lovelace's help if we are to begin testing the ground for anything that might be hidden. Come on!"

The young man headed off toward the knight, who was sitting on the far side of the grove beside one of the stones. Simon cut straight across the clearing with Juno following closely behind, and was looking around the open space for any new sign of the stone container, when suddenly he fell forward and tumbled into the flowers.

"Are you unharmed, lad?" called out the knight without getting up.

"Yes," Simon answered as Juno arrived and helped him to his feet. "I must have tripped over something."

Looking at the ground the way he had come, Simon could not seem to find the obstacle he had stumbled over. But as he searched the ground in the center of the clearing more carefully, he noticed something neither of the others had yet to find. It seemed that rather than trip, Simon had fallen because the ground beneath his feet changed elevation.

"What is it, Simon?" Juno asked.

"The ground," he began. "I seem to have fallen into a small depression. I did not see it before because of all the flowers growing here. But if I walk carefully and feel about with my boots, I can clearly find the outline of a round depression."

Juno stepped down to join him as Sir Lovelace walked over. "Yes, I can feel the drop-off as well," she said. "It is as if something large had once sat here, and left an impression in the ground when it was removed."

"That would have been one large object," the knight offered, standing over them. If indeed it was the stone container you two were told about, it would have been a very large stone. Something like that would not simply walk off on its own and vanish."

"No," Simon replied suddenly. "No it would not. It would have been carried away intentionally."

Juno looked at Simon curiously. "Do you know something we do not?" she asked.

Simon stared at the barely visible impression in the flowers and then glanced toward the forking river. An idea was beginning to form in his mind that seemed utterly amazing. And although it seemed far too uncanny to be true, if there was anything his journey had taught him thus far it was that sometimes the most obvious answer is the most unexpected.

"What is it, lad?" the knight asked with a concerned look on his face. "Well go ahead then. Speak!"

"It is only an idea. A guess. But something deep within my gut tells me I am correct. I think I know where the container was taken."

"You do?" replied Juno and Sir Lovelace simultaneously. The two looked quizzically at each other.

"Yes," Simon answered. "The stone that would have filled this depression in the ground would have looked remarkably similar to another stone I have seen before. One that I have walked past countless times in my life."

"What stone?" the knight asked. "What are you talking about?"

"You have seen it as well, Sir Lovelace," Simon responded. "In Bywood. Do you not remember?"

"I am afraid I do not," said the knight. "Out with it, lad. What are you talking about?"

Simon smiled as he replied, proud of himself for discovering the answer that eluded the others. "We must return to Bywood," he said excitedly. "I believe the lost stone container is the Maidenstone!"

Chapter 18

The sun was high in the sky when the three travelers crossed the border into Bywood from the south. As they made their way out of the edge of the forest and into the well-tended land behind a row of homes, Simon was surprised to notice that it was, of all places, the very home he was raised in that stood before them.

They made their way around the side of the dwelling as quietly as they could, but going unnoticed would be impossible in the full light of day. Simon was beginning to wish that they had waited for nightfall before entering the village, but Sir Lovelace was insistent that they make haste.

At first the few townspeople who were out and about in the hot noon sun did not notice the three strange figures walking toward the street. But as they neared the road that separated the homes from the square at the center of town, a pair of elderly women passed them and left hurriedly, whispered excitedly to each other after recognizing both Simon and the older knight.

It was only after Simon had crossed the street and reached the edge of the square that he heard the sound of a door opening behind him. He turned back to see Eustace Kendrick, the man he had thought of all his life as his father, standing in the doorway of his shop. During the brief moment of eye contact Simon could see the man's face soften with a look of remorse. And then, slowly, Mr. Kendrick retreated into the safety of his workshop.

"What is it, Simon?" Juno asked, placing a hand on his arm. "Who was that man?"

Simon turned to look at her. "Just someone I used to know," he replied.

"Let us keep moving, please," Sir Lovelace suggested forcefully. The others gave him a quizzical look, but set off in the direction of the center of the square.

The rest of the walk to the Maidenstone felt longer than any other time he had made the trip. The square was empty, and all of the signs of the festival held so recently had vanished as well. Simon felt alone in the center of the village he once called home, and realized that nothing had changed.

Simon stepped up to the stone and placed his hands on it, feeling the coolness of the rock and the smooth surface, worn down over centuries of weather and festivals. Memories of his rejection at the hand of Margaret Chilton seemed lost in the distant past now after the adventures that he had experienced since leaving Bywood.

"This standing stone has been at the center of the village, and my life, for as long as I can recall," he said, still studying the lines and coloring of the rock. "Is it not amazing to think of how true that has turned out to be?"

When no one answered, he turned to see if his companions were still there. What he found, though, shocked him. Sir Lovelace had pulled Juno in tight against his chest and was holding the blade of his sword, the sword Simon had returned to the knight, against her throat. Juno was visibly distressed, but she seemed unwilling to cry out with the sharp blade set against the flesh of her neck.

"Give me the key, lad," the knight ordered without emotion. "Hand me the key or she dies right here before your eyes."

Simon was filled with panic. "What are you doing, Sir Lovelace?" he begged. "Let her go!"

"The key," he repeated, more forcefully this

time. Juno was standing perfectly still, but the knight shifted the sword slightly to emphasize his request, causing her to whimper quietly.

"But why?" he asked desperately.

"I recognized that key the moment you showed it to me in the Foxglove Inn before the festival," the knight replied. "I cannot begin to tell you how long I have sought to find it, and after all this time it practically fell into my lap. Now, I will give you one more chance to give me the key before I end the life of this beautiful girl."

Simon did not like the position he was in, but giving up the key to save Juno's life was clearly the better of the two choices. He reached inside his shirt and found the chain around his neck. Lifting it over his head, he held it out for the knight to take. He could feel the familiar weight of the old iron key as it dangled away from the safety of his hand.

"A wise choice, lad," the knight said as he quickly took the key and backed away. After briefly inspecting the key he shoved a distraught Juno to one side and then stepped toward the Maidenstone. Simon rushed over to the nymph to see if she was unharmed while the knight studied the stone while keeping his sword pointed toward them.

"Are you alright?" he asked with obvious concern. She had fallen onto her side, and he leaned down and hooked an arm around her waist and helped her to her feet.

"Yes," she replied, "thank you. What a treacherous thing for him to do, Simon. We have lost the key!"

"I know," he whispered so that the knight could not hear him. "I am open to suggestions on how to get it back, though."

Sir Lovelace was tall enough to reach the stone with ease, and leaned against it to reach over and slide his hand in search of the hole.

"Ah, here it is," he exclaimed as his hand found the small opening at the top of the stone. It was the hole that the villagers had used for generations to hold the post around which the maidens danced each spring during the festival.

"Step away from the stone," came a strong, calm voice from the north.

Simon looked up to see a dark figure stepping out from behind a large oak a few paces from them. The man appeared to be dressed in black from boot to neck, with little decoration or adornment breaking the monotony of his attire.

But his silver mask was what startled him the most. The bearded face cast in silver shone bright below a most unusual helm of black iron and twisted antlers.

Sir Lovelace paused. "Ah," he said. "I see King Telarius has sent his newest Hunter to steal from me what I have rightfully earned."

"I think we would both agree that you are exaggerating your rights ever so slightly," the man in black responded as he stepped closer. "And my orders from King Telarius are, shall we say, complicated, given the current circumstances. I had been seeking a different prize, but apparently my path and yours have been tied more closely than I could have imagined. When I learned that the key had left Bywood, I had a suspicion that you of all people had been involved in that happening. Now that I am certain, I plan to claim what was once mine."

"Yours?" the older knight cried out. "I hardly see how that is possible."

Without a word the Hunter raised a gloved hand and pulled his mask and helm off from his head and tossed them to the side. Beneath the mask was a pale face with a firm jaw and weathered features. Cool blue eyes pierced out from raven hair that hung low over his brow.

"You!" cried out Sir Lovelace. "I thought I killed you!"

"You were mistaken, then," the man replied. "You may have wounded me, but you certainly failed to present a corpse to your master. Tell me, how long did it take before the King removed your cloak and helm and exiled you from his lands?"

"Wait," Simon interrupted. "You were a Hunter, Sir Lovelace?"

"The best there ever was," he replied arrogantly. "But the rules of the position are severe, and I failed to defeat an opponent in single combat. Because of that, I was stripped of my title and banished from Varelia."

"The rules are also clear," added the dark-haired man, "that if a Hunter fails to defeat his opponent, that opponent can be named Hunter by the King."

"True," Lovelace replied. "More intriguing to me than how you became the King's Hunter, however, is how the prize that I desired more than anything else, and sacrificed my position of power to obtain, managed to make its way from your hands to those of this boy."

Simon had been able to follow the conversation clearly up until this moment, but with those words he was suddenly very confused. His key once belonged to the mysterious man with the antlered helm? But he was told that his father had passed it down to him before dying. Unless...

"Simon possessed the key because I gave it to him the night he was born," the Hunter replied. "The very same night you failed to kill me."

"Very clever of you to hide the key with a child," Sir Lovelace spat back. "Did you always know that the key would lead you to the crown?"

"No," the Hunter replied. "It was never clear to me what the key's true purpose was. Handed down to me through a line of ancestors dating back centuries, it was only ever spoken of as a treasure to guard and protect. The King sent me to find the crown, as he has done with every Hunter before me no doubt, but I did not know that my quest would bring me full circle."

"Telarius did indeed task me with the very same mission," Sir Lovelace said. "But he was unaware that I had followed the trail to a key in the possession of a young couple living deep in the Aldwode. I had served my master faithfully for many years, but I felt it was time for me to take the opportunity I saw presenting itself. With the crown, I could usurp the throne and bring glory back to Varelia."

"A shame, then," taunted the Hunter, "that you failed in your scheme." He stepped another pace closer, his hands moving slowly into his flowing black cloak.

"It is of no consequence," the knight bit back, "because I now possess the key. And I find it quite fortuitous that you have returned so that I may finish what I started so long ago."

The knight brought his sword around and held it in front of himself. The Hunter responded by freeing his arms from within his cloak and drawing a pair of simple daggers, which he held out away from his body. Simon was overwhelmed by the details of the conversation, leaving him standing too close to the impending violence. It took only a moment for Juno to realize this and pull him farther away to safety.

Simon heard murmurs behind them and turned to find villagers drifting into the square to discover what the strangers were doing. Some of the women held hands over their mouths in horror at the sight of the violence and conflict they saw brewing before them. To Simon the gathering crowd was like a sea of familiar faces, each representing a life he wished to leave behind, and yet found comfort in.

"Ha!" Sir Lovelace cried out as he leapt forward, swinging his blade upward toward the Hunter's shoulder. The man in black stepped aside smoothly and allowed the older knight to stumble forward before placing a firm kick against his lower back. Lovelace grunted but remained on his feet.

"The King trains his Hunters well," he said, spinning around and bringing the sword back up in defense.

The Hunter stood still and waited for the next blow. "He is a demanding ruler who does not tolerate failure, as you yourself know," he replied with a grin.

Sir Lovelace growled in anger and lunged again, this time bringing his blade down hard toward the Hunter's chest. But again his target moved, stepping to the right while bringing one of his blades around quickly to graze the knight's shoulder.

"You are playing games with me, Hunter," the older man said. "But I do not think you understand how much we are alike. I have faced greater challenges."

"Then I look forward to seeing what you are capable of," replied the man in black.

"Stop it!" Simon cried out. "Why did you give me the key? I need answers. Stop fighting!"

But the two men were locked in combat and unaware of anything else around them. Even the growing crowd of villagers had gone unnoticed as they danced around each other with their weapons drawn. Simon was forced to wait for his answers.

Sir Lovelace moved again, spinning around and bringing the sword with him like a whirlwind. The Hunter ducked and spun to sweep the feet out from under his opponent, but this time the knight moved faster. As he came around he stopped the sword short of his target and rotated further to allow him to swing his free hand with him. A small dagger in that fist caught the Hunter in the upper arm, eliciting a sharp cry of pain.

Sir Lovelace backed away, smiling, and appeared to savor the moment. The Hunter quickly stood, his hand pressed against the wound on his arm, and caught Simon's eye as he turned. For a brief moment the man seemed to smile warmly at him, and then quickly returned to the battle. But for Simon it felt as if something important had just taken place.

"Juno," he said, turning to face her. "What if my father did not die?"

"What?" she replied.

"Everything else about my past has been a lie, so why not the death of my father? What if he was wounded because Sir Lovelace attacked him? What if..."

"...this man is your father!" she finished for him. "Simon, he needs to win this battle if you are to truly discover who you are and who you are meant to be. We need to help him."

"How?" he replied. "I have no weapon. I have never even fought with someone else like this before. I think this is beyond us, Juno."

A loud crash interrupted their conversation, and they turned to see the Hunter fall to the ground, Sir Lovelace standing over him. Blood was slowly running from a wound across the Hunter's chest.

"Get up and fight me," the knight urged. "I will finish what I began so many years ago, and then I will kill your son."

The air grew still but for the soft murmurs of a handful of villagers who understood what he meant. Simon understood the knight's words as well, and knew they were true, but he waited silently for a response from the Hunter to help give life to his hope. The notion that his father was still alive all these years seemed too good to be true.

The man in black rolled and pushed himself to his feet, placing a bloody hand on the Maidenstone to steady himself. He glanced over his shoulder for a moment at Simon before turning again to face the knight. His features had become stern and hard, the muscles in his jaw flexing tightly under his weathered skin.

"I will expend every measure of my strength to prevent that from happening, Lovelace," he hissed in reply. Standing tall, he removed his hand from the stone, leaving behind a red stain.

Instantly the Hunter was loose, leaping forward and bringing both blades upward toward the knight's chest. Sir Lovelace deflected the blows with a swing of his sword, but it was clear to Simon how difficult it was. As the knight staggered backward, his opponent slipped both hands back into his cloak, and when they reappeared the knives had vanished, replaced by a slender blade with elegant curved lines.

The Hunter brought another volley of

attacks against the knight, forcing him back around toward the stone until finally the older man was pressed hard against it. Simon watched as the man in black, the man he had just discovered to be his father, stepped in quickly, dodging a thrust from the knight, to place his sword firmly against the man's throat.

"Yield," he shouted. The crowd around them gasped.

"What?" Sir Lovelace replied, surprised by the offer.

"Yield," the Hunter repeated. "Drop your blade and step away. I have no desire to kill. Just leave us the key and go. You can leave freely if you leave immediately, and never return."

The older knight seemed to consider the offer carefully, and his face spoke of both relief and regret. He slowly let the sword slip from his hand and fall to the ground, where it clanked against the stone before falling into the grass. The chain and key followed, falling to the ground like a metallic, slithering snake.

"Leave now," the Hunter spat at him, stepping back. "You will not receive the luxury of this offer, should we meet again."

Sir Lovelace let his shoulders drop in defeat

and turned to leave while the Hunter looked back at Simon and offered a grim smile. For a moment Simon felt relief at the completion of his quest, but suddenly chaos erupted again. Sir Lovelace spun on his heels and swung the small dagger he still held in his hand toward the Hunter's back.

"Look out!" shouted Juno. The wood nymph tackled Simon from behind and sent him tumbling to the ground just as the blade sped through the air where his head had been moments before. Then the knight bolted toward the crowd.

The Hunter moved instinctively. Even as Sir Lovelace ran away from him, he brought one of the knives out from his cloak again, and with a well-placed throw he struck his target between the shoulders, bringing the man's limp body to the ground.

Chapter 19

The Hunter slowly walked toward Simon and Juno, and Simon could feel his stomach twist with emotion. Juno squeezed his hand as the older man stopped a pace away and smiled.

"I did not think that I would ever see you again, Simon," he said.

"I only just learned that you existed a few days ago, but I was told you were dead." Simon was torn between joy and anger, and his voice shook as he spoke.

"I nearly was," the Hunter replied. "Your mother died giving birth to you that night, giving my heart a mortal wound to match the one Lovelace had given me. But after stumbling back into the forest to die, something happened."

"What do you mean?" Simon asked.

"We found him," interrupted Juno. "My sisters and I. He was the wounded and dying man that stumbled into our grove."

"You—?" Simon asked.

"Yes," she answered. "We provided what care we could and healed his wounds."

"She is correct," the Hunter replied. "Though I do not remember your face, I do remember the kindness you and your people showed toward me."

"But why did you not return for me?" Simon asked with pain in his voice.

"Because," he replied, motioning toward the lifeless body of Sir Lovelace, "he would have followed me and killed us both. I stayed away to keep you safe. And to protect the key."

The Hunter suddenly fell silent and glanced over Simon's shoulder. Simon turned around to see Eustace Kendrick, the man who had reluctantly raised him, walking over to them. His face was pale and serious, but his eyes seemed troubled.

"Simon," the man said plainly, as if merely naming those present.

Simon nodded and forced a respectful nod. The Hunter stepped forward and extended a hand.

"You have aged well, sir," he offered. "Thank you for watching over my son these long years. What you have done is truly selfless."

Mr. Kendrick seemed to squirm under the

weight of the words. He glanced nervously over his shoulder, and Simon could see the bitter, twisted face of Mrs. Kendrick waiting at the edge of the crowd.

"I simply tried to do what seemed right," the cobbler replied. "Will you be needing anything further from us?"

The Hunter seemed taken aback, and Simon felt a small pain in his chest. The Kendricks made it seem so easy to pass him off to someone else and carry on with their lives. He never understood how very little he truly meant to them until now.

"No," he replied firmly. "Thank you for kindly offering."

Eustace Kendrick did not reply, but simply nodded his head ever so slightly, turned around and walked away. Simon watched his former parents disappear into the crowd and suddenly felt very unsure of who or what he was supposed to become.

"Are you ready to become who you were meant to be, Simon?" the Hunter asked him, almost as if he were reading his thoughts.

"What?" he managed to reply.

"Your birthright," the man continued,

motioning toward the standing stone. "You are the one the key was safeguarded for, Simon. The only person with the right to claim the crown as your own."

"But what of the King, and your quest?" Simon asked.

"My quest has changed," he answered. "You see, when I was sent forth from Varelia to find the crown, I did not realize that my path would lead me to the key I once guarded. The very same key I passed to you when you were born.

"For hundreds and hundreds of years, that key has been kept safe within our family. We are descended from the first guardian of the key, Sir Hector, the chief knight of King Toren himself. And Sir Hector was tasked with keeping the key safe until the day when it was needed most. Someone would arise, it was said, who would discover the key's true purpose. But no one expected the key to be part of the larger mystery surrounding the crown of Toren.

"When King Telarius sent me to find the crown I simply expected a challenging quest that would lead me to the crown's hiding place. But instead it led me to the key. And to you, Simon."

"I understand," he replied. "At least, I

think I do. But the crown is not mine to claim. The King is descended from Toren, so the crown belongs to him. I am just the son of a Hunter."

"And the son of a Princess as well," his father replied with a smile.

"I am what?"

"Your mother," he answered, "who died after giving birth to you, was the daughter of King Telarius. She fled her father's rule to be with me years before you were born. Therefore, Simon, you are the grandson of the King as well as the heir to the key that guards the crown. There is no one else who has more right to claim it than you."

The Hunter stepped back over to the standing stone and searched the grass for the key. Finding it, he then returned to Simon.

"Take it," he said. "It is yours, Simon. This is your destiny."

Simon glanced at the ancient key and felt relief to have it back in his hand. Then, with the others watching him closely, he stepped over to the Maidenstone and reached up to find the hole. He slipped his hand inside and found the bottom to the opening, along with a small slit cut into the stone.

The keyhole.

Retrieving the key from his other hand, he repeated the task, but this time he slipped the key into the hole cut for it within the stone and rotated it. It refused to turn at first, but with a bit of forceful twisting Simon managed to cause the lock to engage. A loud crack suddenly emanated from the stone, and Simon jumped away quickly to join the others, bringing the key with him.

The surface of the stone suddenly blossomed with thin, angular fissures, and it appeared that a dim light was pouring through them. The glow within the cracks grew brighter until Simon was forced to shield his eyes. And then, as quickly as it had begun, the light ceased to leak through the lines in the stone, and the Maidenstone crumbled into a pile at their feet.

"Look at that," The Hunter exclaimed, pointing to the center of the rubble.

Amidst the fragments of broken stone stood a small pillar upon which was set a crown. It was far from elaborate or regal; the lines were simple, decorations were few and the metal itself seemed old and weathered. It looked every bit like a relic from a forgotten age.

Simon stepped forward and picked the crown up. It was heavier than it appeared, and he could not imagine wearing it upon his head. For now he was content to simply bring it back to hold up in front of his father and Juno.

"So," he began, "this is mine?"

Juno smiled at him. "It is, Simon. And I am glad it is in your hands and not someone else's."

"Hunter!" came a shout from the north side of the square, interrupting them.

Simon turned to see a small figure moving their way slowly. It appeared to be a woman. As she drew closer, Simon became more and more certain he had seen her before. But before he could recall where, the Hunter spoke up.

"What are you doing here, witch?" he growled at her.

"Witch?" Simon wondered aloud. "She is the woman who told my fortune in the Aldwode!"

The remaining villagers crowded around them parted to let the old woman pass through. She was grinning, and seemed to have a bounce in her step that Simon did not recall from before. She was just as he had remembered her, otherwise, with her plain brown skirt and oddly shaped basket tucked under one arm.

"I remember both of ya," she said, eying them with a grin on her face. "I remember helping the both of ya, too, I do."

"You gave me words and empty legends, Hekate," the Hunter replied spitefully. "The only aid you provided was to point me to the dragon's lair."

"Aye, that I did," she nodded. "And you," pointing a crooked finger at Simon, "I gave you something as well, did I not?"

The young man remembered the moment in the forest well. "She told my fortune," he said. "But so much of it was nonsense. I did not understand what her words meant."

"But you heard them, did ya'not, lad?" The witch leaned forward, smiling.

"Yes," he replied.

"So you might also remember the promise of payment, then," she suggested. "Payment for my gift to you."

"What is she talking about?" the Hunter interrupted. "Simon, you did not strike a bargain with a witch, did you? There is no one more deceptive, and deceitful, than a witch. What exactly happened?"

Simon began to worry. "She demanded payment for my fortune, but I had nothing to pay her with, so she asked for a favor at a later time."

"What was the favor?" his father pressed. "Simon, what did you agree to give her?"

"Oh, Simon," Juno whispered mournfully. "What have you done?"

Simon swallowed as he realized the significance of the deal he had agreed to with the witch. He looked at his father and suddenly felt horribly guilty.

"She said I would bring defeat to the Hunter. She asked for the soul of the Hunter as payment." He could barely speak the words.

"Yes," grinned the witch as she practically shook with glee. "And now I have come to claim my payment, Hunter." Her eyes seemed hungry now.

The Hunter stood silently for a moment, his brow creased with thought. Simon had inadvertently given away the greatest gift he had ever received. Could the power of the crown somehow end the bargain and set the Hunter free?

"A deal is a deal, witch," the Hunter finally said. "And so you shall receive your payment."

The witch clapped her hands together with joy and seemed ready to enjoy a large feast. But then the Hunter interrupted her celebration.

"You may have your Hunter," he offered,

and then pointed to the body of Sir Lovelace laying face-down in the grass near the crowd. "And there he is. Claim his soul before it departs and leaves this realm forever."

"What?" she cried out. "But you are the Hunter, not he!"

"They both are," said Juno, correcting the witch.

"She is right," Simon added as he began to understand his father's plan. "Sir Lovelace was the Hunter who served the King before my father. That was something he was very proud of, to be sure."

The Hunter smiled at his son. "You see, witch, your demands never specified that it must be me that you take. You simply requested a Hunter. And there he lays, freshly killed and ready for you. Now take your payment and go, before my son, the new King of Varelia, tests the power of his crown.

Hekate choked back her words and stared at the dark iron crown Simon held in his hand. Then she slowly backed up and turned toward the body, as if she realized how foolish it would be to disagree with them.

The witch set her basket on the ground beside the body of Sir Lovelace, removed the rags from the opening and then lowered herself slowly to her knees. For a moment she did not move, but then Simon began to hear the sound of something low and guttural. A chant, less musical than painful in tone, began to spill from her lips as the crowd of people near them grew silent.

After a few moments had passed by, a mist began to form over the wound in the back of the dead knight's head. Then, Hekate slowly wrapped her hand around the knife that was embedded in the body and pulled it free. As she did so, the mist grew more dense and expansive, and seemed to flow from the wound itself.

Simon watched in amazement as the witch wove her fingers through the mist, bending and gathering the whisps like thread. Slowly all the strands were drawn toward her and wrapped around her hand, disconnecting from the body. And then, quickly, she pushed the mysterious bundle into her basket and pushed the rags back in place.

"Now that you have what you came for," the Hunter said, "it is time for you to leave us. Be gone!"

Without a word the old woman turned and walked quickly toward the wall of villagers. A moment later she was gone, like a mist into the air.

"Well that was closer to death than I ever want to get," the Hunter announced. "Now that we have settled that matter, let us discuss the next step on your journey, Simon. It is time you claimed the throne."

Simon nodded, but he felt numb. He had been the poor son of a cobbler just a handful of days prior, and now he was holding the Iron Crown, the source of the legendary King Toren's power, and making plans to take control of a kingdom. It was almost too much to take in at once.

"Of course this means that you now must travel to Varelia," the Hunter added. "There is a man upon the throne who will not be happy with how this quest has ended. But I will go with you to provide aid in that transition."

"As will I," added Juno.

"That is very kind of you," Simon replied. "But you have given me more than enough already, and I am forever indebted to you for all you have done."

"It is more than an honor, Simon," she replied. "It has been my duty."

"I do not understand," he said, confused

again. He was beginning to expect surprises and confusion as of late.

"My people have served the land for centuries," she answered. "Though we are not immortal, we do live long lives, and share a special connection with the forests and their sacred groves. And long ago, well before I was born into this world, my people were tasked with safeguarding the Alsean Grove."

"Why that grove?" Simon asked.

"I do not know," she replied. "But by the time I was born my people had moved their focus to a small village, this village, that they guarded diligently. After seeing the Alsean Grove and now the Maidenstone here, I can assume that my people had actually been entrusted with the care of the stone. And the crown."

"I am glad to see that my family is not the only group of guardians who seem to have forgotten their mission over the centuries," the Hunter offered with a weak smile.

"Indeed," Juno replied. "And had it not been for Simon leaving this village I might never have learned the true purpose I had been asked to serve. Now, though, I see that I had not been guarding a place so much as a power. The power of the crown. And as the crown moves north, so must I. No longer will I guard this village; I will, instead, protect you, Simon."

Simon was overwhelmed with all that had happened since entering the tiny town he once called home. But the wood nymph's words made him feel both honored and cared for, even if much of it was rooted in an ancient directive to protect the crown. Whatever the reasons, Simon's past had led him straight into a hopeful future, and he was glad that he would not have to face it alone.

"Then I welcome your company, Juno," he finally said. "And yours...father."

The Hunter smiled at Simon's words. "That is an odd word to utter, is it not? I still have a difficult time believing that I have been reunited with my son."

"We have quite a bit to catch up on, I suppose," Simon replied. "Thankfully we have a long journey north to make up for lost time."

With crown in hand and belongings gathered, Simon, his father and Juno made for the north side of the square. They soon took to the North Road, and Simon glanced back one last time on the village he had called his home. But try as he might he could not imagine a moment as bright and wonderful as this. And as he left his past behind him in pursuit of a hopeful future, he smiled knowing that the best was yet to come.

Epilogue

All roads have a beginning, an origin, a nexus. Sometimes that beginning is found within a magnificent city full of delicate spires and sprawling, well-tended shops. Other roads seem to be born out from the dust and dirt of some nearly forgotten, sorely neglected hamlet far from the rest of the known world. But no matter the source, the quality of the stone or the depth of the grooves worn into them through use and years, every road has an end.

And so it is with tales, as well. For while some might begin with hope and life, and others from the midst of pain and despair, every tale comes to a close. For Simon, we might imagine that leaving Bywood with the crown of Toren in hand, reunited with his father and in the company of a loyal friend was the moment his story found completion, but in this we would be wrong. Simon's tale, you see, had only just begun.

After leaving Bywood behind and traveling

into the Aldwode, the trio of travelers set off to find the River Estin so that they might follow it north toward Varelia. Before continuing onward, however, they traveled east toward the lair of the Red Drake upon Simon's insistence. He had, it seemed, unfinished business to attend to there.

Though it pained the dragon greatly to agree to the terms of Simon's request, he did so out of honor to the promise he had made, and out of allegiance to the new King of the Varelian Empire. From that day forth no raid or attack was ever committed by the dragon upon the dwarves of Fel'nagast.

The King of the Dwarves, though initially doubtful that Simon would keep his word, rejoiced at the news and ordered a celebration for his people that encompassed a long and eventful fortnight. And once the feast came to a close the King sent gifts and offerings of peace to the new Iron King, and both kingdoms enjoyed a long and storied friendship that was both fast and fierce.

By Simon's request, the stone fragments of the Maidenstone that sat in the center of the square in Bywood were gathered up by the monks of the abbey and taken to the crown's original resting place beneath their central tower. After housing the powerful crown for many centuries it seemed that the stones had retained a small amount of magic for themselves, and it was decided that keeping them safely guarded was better than leaving them to fate.

Upon returning to his position of power in the walls of the palace high upon the mountain, the Hunter renounced his helm and secrecy, choosing instead to serve openly as Simon's counselor and aid. Herian, for that was his name by birth, was also the one to remove Telarius from power, offering the former ruler a chance to leave the palace peacefully, an offer which the old man gladly accepted.

As a ruler, Simon learned quickly and in time won over the hearts of the citizens of Varelia. The power of the crown and the purity of his ancestry served to command respect and loyalty from every territory in the realm, and as the years passed the Varelian Empire was restored to the former glory only known before in legends. He became known as Simon the Unifier, and his reign was considered to be the beginning of one of the brightest ages in the history of Varelia.

Juno did not long serve as guardian and protector of the crown and king, however. Shortly after settling into the palace and adapting to her new life there it became clear that she and Simon were destined for more than friendship. Within the year the pair were married and together they filled the cold stone halls of the palace with life and laughter.

Every tale that has a beginning also has an end. And while some travelers hope that rewards or riches await them at their destination, for Simon the outcome was much different. His destiny was not found upon arrival at the end of the road, but along the way, proving that while the ending may be sweet, it is the journey that truly makes us who we are.

ABOUT THE AUTHOR

Aaron Mahnke was born in Illinois in 1975, holds a degree in psychology from Eastern Illinois University, and has built a successful career telling stories for businesses through marketing and design communication. He is a lover of fantasy and science fiction, and a student of history and religion. He currently lives in the Boston area with his wife and two daughters where he is at work on his next novel.

Visit www.aaronmahnke.com to learn more and to sign up for exclusive content and future book release announcements.

Made in the USA
San Bernardino, CA
03 November 2017